POACHERS
BEWARE!

THE RUGENDO RHINOS SERIES

POACHERS BEWARE!

SHEL ARENSEN

Kregel
Publications

To my parents, Ed and Esther Arensen.
Thanks for giving us Africa as our home.
And thanks, Dad, for hunting trips on the plains.
May those memories never fade.

CHAPTER ONE

MOVIE TALENT SCOUT

Someone shoved me against Jill Artberry as our fifth-grade class formed a line to go into the cold school assembly hall. Her long honey-colored hair swept into my nose as she turned around to see who had bumped into her. "Sorry," I mumbled.

She rewarded me with a smile that turned my big ears red. "It's OK," she said. "I wonder what this special assembly is all about?"

I shrugged. "Who knows? Who cares, as long as I get a break from math? I hate long division."

Just then the line started moving. We shuffled into the assembly hall and sat down on the icy metal seats. Mr. Rayford, the principal, sat on the platform with a man wearing a bright orange shirt printed with flowers. A flat gold chain lay around his neck, and he wore sunglasses even in the building.

The sixth-graders moved into the row behind us, and a voice whispered in my ear, "Who's the weirdo in the sunglasses?" I recognized the voice of Matt, my best friend and the captain of our Rugendo Rhinos club. I started to answer but a glare from both of our teachers halted our conversation.

Jon and Dave sat in the row ahead of me with the fourth-grade class. Dave's glasses leaned to the right like a sagging broken ladder. He pushed them straight and turned and winked at me. The four of us, together with Kamau, who attended the nearby Kenyan primary school, were all members of the Rugendo Rhinos club. We had named our club after those two-horned dinosaur-like animals that still roam Kenya's drylands. We loved all wild animals and the fast-disappearing rhino was a symbol of Kenya's endangered wildlife.

Matt Chadwick, our leader, was a year older than the rest of us. He had suggested we build a tree fort for our clubhouse. Dave Krenden was our builder and also acted as our treasurer. He designed the tree fort in a massive wild fig tree. Jon Freedman, our bushmaster, lived for tracking and hunting animals. He loved the woods and could locate pigeons or duikers while the rest of us were trying to unhook ourselves from wait-a-bit thorns without having the fishhook-like barbs tear big hunks of flesh out of our arms or legs. My name is Dean Sandler, and I'm the official Rugendo Rhino secretary. Kamau, the fifth member of our Rhino club, is a Kenyan boy. He turned into our club's prayer warrior after a near-death demonic attack in one of our earlier adventures.

Kamau wasn't at our missionary kids' school assembly because he attended a Kenyan primary school on the mission station called Rugendo where we all lived.

My dad, who edited a Christian magazine, gave me the idea of writing down our adventures. Once Matt had been kidnapped after we had stumbled onto a secret oathing ceremony, and we'd had to rescue him. We also put a gang of carjackers out of business. We had forests to explore, games to play, bikes to ride, and we loved all of it. Except for school. Who wanted to be trapped in a classroom when we could hear turacos, large blue and red forest birds, churring in the forest?

Mr. Rayford stood up now and cleared his throat. Maybe it was my imagination, but he almost sounded like a turaco. "Today I've called an assembly," he began, "because we have a special guest. Mr. Harris works with the movies in Hollywood, and he has come to our school to make an exciting announcement."

Mr. Harris stood up. I wondered how he could see in the gloomy assembly hall with those sunglasses, but he didn't stumble as he stepped to the microphone. "I'm a talent scout," he said. "My company is planning to film a movie here in Kenya. We're trying to raise the world's awareness of the fragile ecology and the threat to Africa's wild animals. The movie is about poachers, an orphaned cheetah, and a conservationist who is trying to protect the animals. We'll shoot most of the movie in the savannah plains on the floor of the Rift Valley near Mount Suswa." He paused.

I glanced out the window at the sharp edge of Mt. Suswa's giant crater rim in the tawny valley below Rugendo. He had my full attention. We'd often driven to Suswa to explore the lava tube caves. They would film a movie at our volcano? I wondered what kind of talent he was looking for. Could he use us Rhinos?

Mr. Harris went on, "Most of the actors and actresses for the movie have already been chosen back in the States and will arrive in Kenya soon. But I'm looking for a young person who lives here in Kenya and can speak Swahili. I've already visited some schools in Nairobi. This is my last stop. I'll be holding tryouts here in your assembly hall after school today. I'll be looking for acting ability and a good knowledge of Swahili. Both boys and girls are welcome. I hope some of you will come and try out for a part in this movie."

With that he sat down. A low murmur like the sound of a small waterfall filled the room. "I'm going to try out," I whispered over my shoulder to Matt.

"Me, too," he said, his corn-colored hair falling into his eyes. *"Mimi ninajua Kiswahili sana.* I know Swahili very well."

"Kamau knows Swahili better than all of us," I said. "I wonder if he'd like to try out?"

"Quiet, please! Quiet everyone," Mr. Rayford waved his arms at us like a band director. The hissing of the whispering tapered off. Mr. Rayford turned to Mr. Harris. "Thank you. I'm sure you can tell from the response that you will have plenty of children trying out. I hope one of our students gets chosen." He straightened up and looked out at us. "This is a wonderful opportunity, children. A chance to be part of a movie that will focus on the plight of Africa's wildlife." He rambled on for a while about our role as Christians to conserve God's creation before giving a few announcements and dismissing us back to class.

As we sat down at our forest green desks, Jill touched my arm. "Aren't you excited about trying out?" she asked.

I nodded. "A bit nervous, too, now that I think about it. What about you? Are you going to try out?"

"I'm not sure I know enough Swahili," Jill admitted. "But I'll give it a try. After all, the movie is about a cheetah. And our club is the Cheetahs."

Jill had started her Cheetah club a few months before when we were trying to solve the mystery of a gang of armed carjackers operating in East Africa. Ever since then, the Cheetahs and the Rhinos have been battling each other to see which club could solve mysteries first. I saw it as a friendly rivalry. For Matt, our honor as an all-boys club was at stake. It galled him to think girls might be better than the Rhino club at anything.

Freddie, another member of the Cheetahs, leaned toward Jill. "Let's all try out for a part in the movie," she said. "Just think, maybe one of us from the Cheetah club could be in a real movie about a cheetah." Freddie's real name was Fredricka Bernhardt and she came from Germany. She climbed trees better than any of the boys in fifth grade. She lived in the dorm during school because her parents worked in Uganda.

"Of course that Hollywood guy will choose one of us," put in Rachel Maxwell from her desk behind us. "We're perfect for the part—missionary kids who feel more at home in Africa than anywhere else in the world."

"But we're all missionary kids. How can we be sure he'll choose one of us Cheetahs?" asked Rebekah, Rachel's older sister. The Maxwell sisters were also part of the Cheetahs. Their parents used to work in the country of Zaire until a rebellion had forced the missionaries to flee for their lives. The country had changed its name to Congo, and the Maxwells worked at the Bible College at Nairobi while waiting for a chance to go back into Congo. Rebekah was older by a year, but during their years of being home-schooled, Rachel had caught up, and they were both in fifth grade and lived in the dorm at school.

"Calm down, children," our teacher hushed, bringing all of us back to earth by passing out another worksheet on long division.

"Who cares what 1,488 divided by 24 is anyway," I mumbled as I started working on the first problem. In my concentration, I pressed too hard with my pencil and the point broke off. I went to the teacher's desk to sharpen it and had to wait while Freddie worked on her pencil first. She twirled the sharpener handle wildly and snapped the lead three times before she got her pencil sharp. She blew off the shavings and stepped aside. I didn't mind watching Freddie mess with her pencil, since I knew what waited for me back at my desk.

After math, the day improved with reading. I loved reading, and the story in our book was a true one about Joy Adamson, a lady from Kenya who adopted a baby lion cub, which she called Elsa. The story told how she'd managed to teach Elsa to hunt and return back to the wild. When our teacher asked us to discuss what we read, I put my hand up.

"Last month my parents took me to visit Elsamere on the edge of Lake Naivasha. It used to be Joy Adamson's home and now it's a conservation center that works to save Africa's animals."

When Matt leaned out of the sixth-grade door and rang the large hand bell to signal the end of the day, I ran out to meet him. He was just putting the bell away. Each week a different sixth-grader had the job of ringing the bell. Matt rang it harder than anyone. He had a big smile on his face when he saw me. "Let's get Dave and Jon," he said. "We'll go try out for a part in this movie. I'm sure he'll want some real bush guys like us."

We found Dave and Jon at the water fountain. Jon finished his drink and squirted Dave in the face. Dave glared steadily at Jon, but said nothing. He slurped down his own drink before carefully taking off his water-beaded glasses and drying them on his white T-shirt.

"I'm going to run get Kamau," I said. "Save us a place in line."

I caught Kamau as he walked out the primary school gate. "Kamau," I called.

"Dean, *jambo*, how are you?" Kamau said, turning to shake my hand.

"Come quick. There's a man from Hollywood at our school looking for someone to act in a movie."

"Where's Hollywood?" Kamau asked, puzzled.

"I'll explain while we walk. We have to hurry so we won't be late."

When Kamau and I arrived at the assembly hall, it seemed that every kid in our school stood in line to audition. We joined the other Rhinos near the back to wait our turn. Jill and the other fifth-grade Cheetahs stood near the front. Jill's little sister Beth, the fifth member of their club, joined them. They looked smug.

"I'll bet Jill and her friends think they'll get a part in this movie," Matt said, snorting as he spoke.

"If they did, there would be Cheetahs in a cheetah movie," I said, pleased at my wit.

Matt frowned. "Sounds like you *want* one of them in the movie," he said. "What are you, anyway? A friend of the Cheetahs? Or maybe we should just call you Jack."

"What do you mean, call me Jack?" I asked.

"Jack and Jill went up the hill . . . " Matt began in a mocking tone.

My face flushed, and I slugged him on the shoulder.

"Ouch!" Matt howled. "That hurt!" Everyone turned around to look at us. Now it was Matt's turn to be embarrassed.

The talent scout looked vaguely in our direction before waving his hand for the next girl in line to come forward. He wrote her name down on his clipboard before looking her over like a slave master examining a new purchase. He looked at her teeth, measured her hair by spans of his hand. He asked her to say something in Swahili before motioning her to leave and calling up the next person as he jotted a few things down on his paper.

"He doesn't seem to be listening very carefully to their Swahili," Matt whispered.

"I don't think he's giving them much of a chance to show their acting skills, either," Dave answered.

"It looks more like a beauty contest," Jon said.

My heart sank. "If it is, I won't have a chance," I said, thinking of my oversize ears, blotchy freckles, and braces.

Jill and her Cheetahs stepped forward one by one. The scout seemed to take a long time with Jill. He even had her repeat her line in Swahili. Even from the back I could hear her clear voice cut through the whispering. *"Je, ungetaka mimi kusema nini,"* which meant, "Hey, what would you like me to say?" Of course the scout's total ignorance of Swahili meant he didn't understand her clever sentence. We all laughed as the scout looked puzzled. He even slipped down his sunglasses to glare at the crowd. After Jill, he began working through the line at lightning speed. He almost ignored Beth and barely glanced at Freddie with her short, ragged haircut.

When it finally got to our turn, he cut Matt off in midsentence, and I didn't even get a chance to say anything. He just looked at me and waved me past. He listened to Kamau speak in Swahili and then nodded.

As soon as the last person had passed by, the talent scout stood up and said, "Thank you all for coming. I believe I can now announce my decision."

THE CHAMELEON

Hardly pausing to give us a chance to listen, Mr. Harris said, "I would like to offer Jill Artberry a part in the film. Could Jill please come speak with me about arrangements." He looked up as Jill began walking slowly to the front. She had a silly smile on her face, but her eyes looked dazed. With a quick flip of his hand, Mr. Harris dismissed the rest of us. "Thank you all for trying out. I'm sorry we didn't have space for more of you." He put his arm around Jill and had her sit down on a chair, and the two began to talk quietly.

Matt and I stood stunned, then turned and wandered out into the playground. "We never had a chance!" Matt snarled. "He just wanted the prettiest girl for the film. I know Swahili better than Jill. So does Kamau. And Jon could have shown off his tracking skills. What a rip-off!" He stopped jabbering to catch his breath. Looking up at the dark forest in the hills above Rugendo, he said, "Let's go for a quick hike to the waterfall. I don't want to think about movies anymore. It will probably be a sissy movie anyway, full of girls and tears and stuff. It's probably better we didn't get chosen."

Kamau agreed. "I'm glad he didn't pick me. I don't know any-thing about films."

Matt marched up the hill, and we followed. We had to walk fast to get to the waterfall and back before dark. We hiked without talking, most of our breath being used to suck in enough oxygen for our lungs. My dad said the Rugendo mission station had been built at seven thousand feet above sea level to avoid malaria. When-ever visitors came they could hardly climb the steps in our house without stopping to catch their breath. We usually didn't feel the lack of oxygen except when we hurried like today.

Arriving at the waterfall, Matt kicked off his shoes and peeled off his Minnesota Twins T-shirt. Wearing just his shorts, he jumped into the pool under the white cascade of water and began floating on his back. We all jumped in after him. The cold mountain water stung our skin and numbed our legs and arms, but it felt good and washed the sweat and dust off our bodies.

"Watch this!" Matt commanded as he scrambled up to a place where a smaller stream of water had cut a channel to the right of the main waterfall. Using the channel like a water slide, Matt sat down and started to slide. He gathered speed, shot off the end, and splashed tail first into the water, leaving a towering spout of water where he landed. "That was great!" Matt shouted as he shook the water out of his hair like our dog after a bath. "You've all got to try it!"

Jon climbed up and launched himself with a loud whoop and splashed into the pool. I looked at Dave. He nodded and started up. "Hurry up, you guys!" Matt called. "It's great!" I hung back. I didn't want to admit the sinking feeling in my gut. I hated speed-ing downhill on a bike. This seemed like it would be even worse, but I couldn't let the others know I was afraid.

"Are you afraid, Dean?" Kamau whispered.

"A little," I admitted.

"Let's go together," Kamau said.

Matt pushed past us. "Move over, Dave," he commanded as he got to the top. "I'm going down again."

Kamau climbed up and I followed. I sat down in the stream behind Dave and Kamau, expecting them to go first. But I must have sat on a slippery spot because I starting sliding and couldn't stop. I bashed into Kamau, who slipped into Dave who was settling himself for a push-off.

"What are you guys doing?" Dave cried, but before I could answer we were airborne. Flying through the air, I felt sure I'd die. We hit the water in a flail of legs and arms before sinking beneath the surface. As we spluttered up, Matt cheered. "A train! Great idea, you guys. Jon, wait for me, and we'll try a train too!"

Jon and Matt linked up like bobsledders and splashed into the water together.

After some more sliding, we lay on our backs on the lush green grass that surrounded the pool. The waning late afternoon sun didn't bite ferociously into our skin like it did at noon, but we could feel the warmth coming back into our numbed bones.

We lay quietly, listening to the birds quirking and kleeping in the forest trees. A large silver-cheeked hornbill flew into a nearby *muthaiga* tree with a clattering noise. Matt stood up to watch. "I wish we could shoot one of those one day. We could stuff it and put it in our tree house."

I preferred live birds flying and honking in the forest, but I didn't say so.

"Hey, what's that?" Matt asked, moving toward a bush covered with yellow flowers. We sat up and watched him. Reaching out to a thin branch, he plucked a small creature from its perch.

"It's a chameleon!" Jon blurted as Matt brought it back for us to admire. "What a beauty!"

"You shouldn't touch it," Kamau said. "Chameleons are bad." That was a traditional African belief.

Matt brushed aside Kamau's advice. "I've touched tons of chameleons," he said, "and they don't seem to bother me."

The rough sides of the chameleon's body had a yellow and green color from the bush where it had been hiding. As it rocked back and forth on Matt's hand, not sure which direction to move, we could see the chameleon's color change to a dull flesh color.

"I've heard that the only color a chameleon can't turn is red. And if you put a chameleon on a red shirt or blanket it will die of the effort to turn red," Dave said.

"Doesn't work," Matt said. "I tried it once. It's true the chameleon doesn't turn red, but it doesn't die. It just moves somewhere else and tries to blend into its surroundings."

Kamau kept his distance. The chameleon wound up its tail in a tight coil like a nautilus shell. Its large protruding eyes rolled back and forth in different directions at the same time.

"Look," I said. "It's looking at me with its right eye, but its left eye is looking backward at Matt's arm."

The chameleon's right front claws yawned open as it searched for a branch where it could escape. Above its pebble-like eyes, three horns pointed forward, making the lizard look like a miniature triceratops.

"It's a Jackson's chameleon," Jon said knowingly. "That's the kind with three horns." He stroked the horns and the chameleon drew back from his touch.

The sun disappeared behind a cloud, and a chilly breeze ruffled the leaves behind us. "Brrr!" Matt said. "It's getting cold. Let's head back to Rugendo. I'm going to take this chameleon home with me. My mom has been complaining about the flies in the house. I'll just put the chameleon in the curtain, and it can catch those flies for my mom with its long sticky tongue."

We put our shirts and shoes on and jogged back toward Rugendo. The shadows grew faster than we could run. My wet shorts began to chafe on the insides of my thighs. "I know a short-cut," Jon called ahead to Matt. Matt stepped aside and let Jon lead the way. "It's a bushbuck trail," Jon said, "so it's a little overgrown, but it will save us almost a mile."

I brought up the rear and tried to avoid whipping slaps from bushes that had been pushed aside by those in front. Suddenly I heard a thump, and Matt's voice cried out, "Jon, are you OK? What happened?"

Dave, Kamau, and I caught up in seconds to see Jon flat on his face, his leg out behind him at an awkward angle. Jon made some wheezy noises out of his mouth and sat up slowly.

"I think I just got the wind knocked out of me," he gasped finally. But his leg still pointed off into the bushes. He dragged himself in the direction of his leg. A rusty wire snare had wrapped itself around Jon's ankle. It had already bitten a hole into his white sock. A circular crimson stain crept slowly down the sock.

"It's a snare for small antelope. Don't pull any harder," I told Jon. "That'll only pull the snare tighter. Our dog Grump almost got killed in this type of snare. She went running after monkeys and got her head caught in a noose snare. She struggled so much that the wire sawed into her neck. It's a good thing we heard Grump howling and found her. My dad cut the wire snare before it strangled her."

"Yeah, that was gross, Dean," Matt said. He knelt and gently eased the snare open and released Jon's leg. Jon rubbed the spot where the wire had cut a small line around his ankle. "It's just a scratch," he said bravely. The sock seemed to blot any bleeding, and Jon stood up and began walking. "It doesn't hurt," he said, but he limped.

Before leaving, Dave uprooted the snare. "I'm taking this home," he said. "It's proof that poaching is coming close to Rugendo."

"I don't think it's professional poachers," I answered. "They usually don't bother with small things like bushbuck. It's probably just some local person who wanted to eat some meat. Kind of like the Dorobo hunter we met during the mystery of the poison arrow tree."

"Sure," Kamau said. "I know some people who trap small antelopes to eat."

We got home just as the fiery red sun dropped behind the rim of Suswa, the old volcanic crater that stood in the valley in front of Rugendo. We dropped Jon off first. His dad, a doctor, clucked at the cut around his ankle and said something about a tetanus shot. We slipped away. Back at home I told my parents about our day—the movie scout, our hike, the chameleon, and the snare that had grabbed Jon's ankle and hurled him to the ground.

My dad frowned at the mention of the snare. "Kenya's wildlife is really under pressure," he said. "The animals don't seem to have many safe places to live. Even on the edges of game parks, poachers are killing elephants. In Meru Game Park, some poachers actually came into the park and killed the white rhinos that were under twenty-four-hour protection by game rangers."

"But, Dad, don't people like the Dorobo depend on their hunting to survive?" I asked.

"That's true," he answered. "People who hunt animals for their food usually aren't the problem, though. The Dorobo only hunt what they can eat. And they don't use modern weapons. Just poison arrows and spears."

"And snares?" I asked.

"Yes, they do use snares," he agreed. "But it's still pretty small-scale stuff. The big concern is poaching operations where they hammer elephants with machine guns, chop the tusks out, and leave the carcass to rot. Others collect horns, skins, and other animal trophies and ship them out of the country for cash. Ever since legal hunting was outlawed in Kenya in the late 1970s, poaching has increased."

"But if people aren't hunting, there should be more animals," I pointed out.

"You'd think so," my dad said. "The purpose of banning hunting in Kenya was to stop poaching. But they have found out that without legal hunters on some of the large blocks of land that were previously set aside for hunting, the poachers have increased. The game department doesn't have enough time, people, or vehicles to cover all the territory. When hunters were allowed in, they only killed a few animals, based on what licenses they had bought. But their very presence in these areas kept poaching down."

"Time to eat," my mom said, interrupting our talk. I put poaching and snares out of my mind as I scarfed down fried chicken and mashed potatoes.

That evening in family devotions my dad read from Psalm 91. "You will trample the great lion and the serpent," he read.

"Does it really say that?" I asked. Dad nodded as I looked over his shoulder. "It sounds like those verses are for us in Africa."

Mom smiled. "You're right, Dean. It says specifically God will protect us from wild animals that we see here in Africa." She prayed for our family.

Afterwards, Dad said, "The chameleon you found today reminded me of a story I heard recently. It tells why so many Africans fear the chameleon. It also explains why people have different colored skin."

"Tell us, Dad, please!" pleaded my little brother, Craig.

He looked at my mom. She smiled and said, "There should be time to tell them a story while their bath water is running." She stood up to start the hot water.

"The story goes like this," my dad began. "A long time ago when God created the world, he created three men. He fashioned them out of the mud of the earth, and all three men were black as the dirt. He left them to dry and went on about the business of creating. Then he remembered the three men. He wanted them to wash the mud off in a certain pool of water. He called the impala, the turtle, and the chameleon and told each one to go to one of the three men and tell them to go and wash.

"The impala ran straight to the first man, who heard the message and went to the pool of water. There he washed all the mud off and became white. That is why there are white people in the world.

"The turtle went as fast as he could, which wasn't very fast at all, until he found the second man. The second man went to wash, but found that much of the pond had disappeared in the hot sun. So he could only wash part of the dirt off. That is why there are brown people in the world.

"The chameleon promptly forgot what God had asked him to do. Some months later, he remembered. In his slow back-and-forth amble, he went to find the third man. When he told the third man to go and wash, the man obeyed at once. But the special pool of water had dried up except for a tiny patch. All he could do was put the soles of his feet and the palms of his hands into the water. That is why there are black people in the world, and why black people have white skin on their palms and on the soles of their feet. And ever since, African people have despised and feared the chameleon."

"That's a good story, Dad," I said. "I'll tell the guys tomorrow. Matt said he'd keep the chameleon on his mom's curtain to keep down the flies."

The next day as I hurried to school, I saw Matt ahead of me. "Matt, wait up!" I called.

He turned, his face split by a huge grin. "You'll never guess what I did with my chameleon!" he said.

CHAPTER THREE

FILMING THE MOVIE

"What?" I asked.

"I told you you'd never guess." Matt smiled at his own cleverness. "Look at this."

He pulled a clear plastic peanut butter jar from his pocket. Inside, five shiny blue-bottle flies buzzed around. Some holes had been punched in the lid of the jar. Matt produced the chameleon from the large pocket of his green fleece jacket. Setting the jar on the ground, Matt held the chameleon on his finger about ten inches away. The flies in the jar settled down. The chameleon's eyes rolled around and then fixed on the jar of flies. Steadying itself, the chameleon suddenly shot out its tongue. The tongue swiftly stretched out and ticked the side of the jar causing the flies to jump and fly crazily around again.

"That's amazing!" I said. "I never knew a chameleon's tongue was so long."

"Me neither," Matt said. "I've decided to call my chameleon Ulimi. My dad said that means tongue in Swahili. After watching Ulimi catching flies in the window last night, I decided to catch some of the flies in a bottle and see what he would do. He keeps shooting at the jar. He doesn't understand about plastic."

Dave and Jon came up the path just as Ulimi launched his tongue again. "I'm going to show him off during recess," Matt said proudly as Jon and Dave oohed over the length of Ulimi's tongue.

At recess, kids swarmed around Matt and his pet chameleon. Jill stood by herself on the edge of the crowd. "Where are the rest of the Cheetahs?" I asked.

"I think they're jealous that I got the part in the movie," Jill said. "They're not talking to me."

"I'm sorry," I replied. "So when exactly do they shoot this movie? And what will your part be?"

"You're really interested?" she asked. "You're not mad that I got the part and not one of the Rhinos?"

I shrugged. "Matt was upset yesterday afternoon, but you know how he gets over things. I think our hike to the waterfalls and finding the chameleon made him forget being mad. I'm glad I didn't get a part in the movie. I'd be scared to death."

Jill nodded. "I kind of know what you mean. I'm a bit scared, too. The man gave me a portion of the script yesterday. I only have a small part. When the main actress in the movie, a girl about our age, goes on safari in Kenya, she adopts an orphaned cheetah that's been found on a game ranch. When she arrives at the game ranch to collect the cheetah, she meets the family that runs the ranch. That's where I come in. I'm the daughter of the family that lives on the ranch. I take the main actress to a fenced yard. I whistle for the cheetah to come. I give the cheetah to the girl, saying one line, 'His name is Duma.'"

"Not much Swahili in that line," I said.

"*Duma* is Swahili for cheetah," Jill said. "But you're right, you really don't have to know Swahili to say it."

"So when will they be filming?" I asked.

"They'll start next week," Jill answered. "But the part I'm in will be filmed the following weekend. It's during our school's midterm. Mr. Harris talked with my parents, and that's when they set the time for that scene."

"If it's at midterm, maybe we can come watch some of the filming," I said. "Didn't he say they were filming out in the Rift Valley at Mount Suswa?"

"That's right," Jill said.

The bell rang to end recess. The crowd around Matt broke up as he gathered his chameleon and bottle of flies.

After school that day, I walked home with Matt. We released some of the flies onto the window, and Matt put Ulimi on the flowered curtains. Within minutes, Ulimi had the satisfaction of scoring a real target and reeling in a fly for dinner.

Matt's dad, who taught at the Rugendo Bible school, walked in.

"Hey, boys!" he called. "I just met a man named Mr. Davies in Nairobi who runs a game ranch on the Ewaso Ngiro River. Instead of having cattle, they just allow wild animals on their ranch. They have a permit to shoot a certain number of animals each year to sell to butcheries and restaurants like the Carnivore in Nairobi, which specializes in wild game meat. He said they have an overabundance of impalas, Thomson's gazelles, and warthogs right now and told me we could go camping there on midterm and do some hunting. We'll have to give most of the meat to the ranch, but he said we could keep some, too. I said we'd be glad to come out and do a bit of hunting, just like in the old days when most of us got our meat from hunting in the valley."

Matt exulted, "A hunting trip! I can't wait." He stopped. "Can

Dean come too? And what about Jon, Dave, and Kamau? We can't leave them behind."

His dad scratched his ear, something he always did when he was thinking. Or when he preached in church and waited for the interpreter to finish with the translation before he plunged in with another sentence. After a few seconds, he said, "I see no problem with that. Maybe you Rugendo Rhinos could go on an all-guys camping trip with your dads."

I couldn't believe our luck! Mr. Chadwick sat down in his chair. "I'll talk with the other dads and organize everything," he said. Matt and I went out to tell Jon and Dave the good news.

Dave and I hiked over to Kamau's house. "Kamau, can you join the rest of us Rhinos on a camping trip to a game ranch?"

"With real wild animals?" Kamau asked. "I'd love to, but I have to get permission from my father."

"He's invited, too," Dave said.

Kamau called his father, and we repeated the invitation. Kamau's father thought for a few moments. "I can't join you. I have to attend a pre-wedding party that weekend. But I will allow Kamau to go if he'll spend extra time watching the goats the next two weekends to make up for when he's away."

"I will, father," Kamau promised.

As the days crept closer to midterm, the plans for the hunting trip came together. We would drive out to the Ewaso Ngiro River Game Ranch on Saturday morning of midterm. It was a long midterm because of a Kenyan holiday, so we wouldn't have to be back to Rugendo until Tuesday night.

On Thursday before midterm my dad and I aired out our tent, sleeping bags, and other camping gear. "I hear Jill's scene in that movie is being filmed tomorrow afternoon," he said. "You kids get out of school at 11 A.M. to start midterm. How would you like to take a picnic out and see the movie set? It's not that often we get a real movie shot right in the valley."

"Can I come, too?" a little voice interrupted. My little brother, Craig, had come up behind us and heard the plan. Dad reached down and picked him up. "You sure can, Craig. We'll pack a family picnic and go out and watch them shooting the movie."

The next morning Jill wasn't in class. She'd been excused to go down to Suswa early for the movie shoot. I ran home after school so we could see the filming. It turned out we weren't the only family who decided to take a picnic lunch out to the movie set. As we ate our lunch under an acacia tree, we could see the dust lines from other cars coming across the valley floor. The Maxwells showed up with Rebekah and Rachel, along with Freddie. They'd gotten over their hard feelings toward Jill for winning the part and had come to cheer their fellow Cheetah along. Jill's parents and Beth had been on the set all day. Dr. Freedman pulled up with Jon, Matt, Dave, and Kamau. I gulped the last of my glass of iced grape Kool-Aid and ran to join the other Rhinos.

We wandered over to the fenced area where a half-grown cheetah stalked back and forth. He seemed bothered by all the activity. Tents and awnings had been set up for the movie actors and actresses, but even with the added shade, the director's face glowed red. He wiped sweat from his forehead with a stained bandana.

They were setting up for Jill's scene. The girl actress who would adopt the cheetah glared at Jill and complained, "I hope you get it right the first time. I'm tired of this hot sun, and I want to go home soon."

"I'll do my best, Siana," Jill said, looking nervous. Her crew of Cheetahs gave her the thumbs up, and Jill smiled.

"I don't like that Siana," Matt said. "When they're done with that scene, I'd like to teach her a lesson."

"What do you mean?" Jon asked.

Matt reached inside his shirt and pulled out Ulimi, the chameleon. "What do you think she'd do if I came up to her and stuck Ulimi in front of her face?"

"Great idea!" Jon said. "I'll bet her scream will be loud enough to be heard back at Rugendo."

The director yelled at everyone to be quiet, and they started filming. Siana and her movie parents bounced up the road in a dark green Land Cruiser. As it pulled up in a cloud of dust, the parents went into a nearby house that was really only the front of a house. Jill came over to Siana and the two walked to where the cheetah, which had been taken out of his fenced cage, sat on its hind legs like a dog. Jill gave a quick whistle, and the cheetah walked toward them. As the two girls petted the cheetah, Jill's voice rang out, "His name is Duma."

"Cut!" the director said. "That should be good enough. I liked it, Jill. You acted like the cheetah really was your pet." Turning to the crew he shouted, "All right, let's set up for the scene where there's a rockslide over the mouth of the cave. Get those Styrofoam rocks over there, and we'll try to finish that scene tonight." He swatted at a fly that circled his head.

"He sure could use Ulimi," Matt joked. "Hey, there's that stuck-up Siana coming over here with Jill."

Jill introduced the actress to the girls. "This is Siana Shane," Jill said. Waving with her hand, Jill went on, "These are my friends

29

from my Cheetah club I told you about. Rebekah, Rachel, Freddie, and my little sister Beth." Siana greeted them as if she were doing some task like washing dishes.

"Let's go get introduced," Matt whispered. He had Ulimi on his right hand and tucked his hand behind his back. I wasn't sure I wanted to be part of what might happen next.

Jill waved us over. Matt, an odd grin on his face, pushed the rest of us ahead. We all shook hands with Siana Shane, the movie actress. I kind of grunted a hello but couldn't think of anything else to say. When it came to Matt's turn, he drew his right hand from behind his back and held it out for Siana to shake.

She put her hand out and stopped. Matt waited for a scream, but it never came. "Oh, what a cute chameleon," Siana blurted. "Can I hold it?"

"Uh, sure, I guess," Matt said uncertainly. "So, you, uh, know what a chameleon is? You sure it didn't scare you at all?"

"It surprised me," Siana said, "but it didn't scare me. I have a lizard collection back home in Malibu. I have a huge iguana named Iggy. And I've got a few chameleons, but none with three horns like this. I read about this kind of chameleon in a book on lizards. It's called a Jackson's chameleon, isn't it?"

"You're right," Matt said grudgingly. "At least that's what Jon says. He's our animal expert."

"I'd love to have a chameleon like this for my collection," Siana said.

Matt surprised all of us by saying, "You can have him if you want. I can always find another. I call him Ulimi, which is Swahili for tongue. He has a long tongue."

"Can I keep him? Really?" Siana asked. "What do you feed him? And don't I need a permit to take him out of the country?"

"I feed it flies," Matt said, ignoring her question about a permit. "I'm sure American flies will be just as tasty for him. All you have to do to take him to America is carry him in your pocket and declare him at customs. Some of our friends took four back to America last year. Just make sure you wear something with big pockets and fill them with live flies so you can feed him on the plane. Chameleons don't like dead flies."

Siana's nose wrinkled at the thought of pockets full of flies, but she took the chameleon. It crawled up her arm and perched on her shoulder. "I don't think I'll take him to America, but I'll enjoy him while I'm here in Kenya. Thanks," she said, heading for her tent.

Jill leaned over to Matt and whispered, "It was really nice of you to bring a present to Siana."

"Well, actually I wanted to scare her after the way she talked to you," Matt admitted.

"I know," Jill said. "At first, I hoped she would scream. She hasn't been very easy to work with, but she sure changed when she saw the chameleon. It looks like we may have a new friend instead of a stuck-up movie actress."

Jill and the Cheetahs went over to Siana's tent to talk. With the chameleon as the icebreaker, they now acted like old friends.

Just then one of the men in charge of the cheetah came running over. "Has anyone seen Duma?" he asked, his eyes roving all over. "We forgot to put him in his pen after the last scene, and I can't find him anywhere!"

THE CHEETAH DISAPPEARS

"**W**hat's going on?" the movie director demanded. "What's this about losing the cheetah? You can't have lost the cheetah! We still have to film some scenes where the cheetah plays a major part!"

"I've searched all over the camp," the animal keeper said, red-faced. "He's not here. Maybe he wanted to be free. Maybe he wanted to go hunting. I've noticed over the past few days how alert he gets when some Grant's gazelle graze near our camp. He stares at the animals and twitches his tail."

"You saw this behavior and didn't take extra precautions?" the director asked sharply.

"It's not my fault!" the animal keeper protested. "The cheetah has never strayed before. I'm sure he's just looking for shade in someone's tent."

Jon and Kamau pushed their way forward into the milling crowd that pressed in to hear the bad news about Duma's escape. "Where'd you see the cheetah last?" Jon asked. "We may be able to track which way he went."

Happy to get away from the furious movie director, the animal keeper took Jon and Kamau toward the area where they'd shot the scene with Jill and Siana. We Rhinos followed, and Jill and the Cheetahs hurried to catch up.

The keeper pointed. "The last I saw him, Duma stood here being petted by the two girls. I figured they'd shoot the scene a few more times, so I slipped away to get a drink."

Jon, who had knelt next to the animal keeper to look for tracks, took a deep breath and wrinkled his nose. "I don't think you went for a cold Coke," Jon said. As we gathered around, even I could smell the whiskey on the man's breath.

His face hardened. "It's none of your business what I've been drinking! I can handle myself. If you start spreading rumors about me, you'll regret it."

Jon glared at him. Kamau scanned the ground. "I can see where Duma walked off in that direction," Kamau said. Bending over as they moved, Jon and Kamau followed the tracks. We had to jog to catch up. Behind us the movie director shouted, "Get the cameras rolling. Try to get a close-up of those boys tracking the cheetah. Who knows, maybe we can use some of this footage and add something in the script about the cheetah being abducted by poachers."

We came to a stunted whistling thorn tree with ping-pong sized black balls on its branches next to the thorns. Shiny black ants crawled out of tiny holes in the black balls. My dad calls them galls and says the ants sting the tree, and these galls grow as a result of the sting. The ants burrow in and use the galls as nests. A slight breeze crept across the plains, making low noises as it passed through the whistling thorn, just like blowing across the top of an empty pop bottle.

Kamau showed us where the cheetah had lain down. "He was

probably looking at some prey," Kamau said. We nodded wisely. I could see where the dust had been disturbed, but for all I could tell the marks could have been made by a goat or a puff adder.

"And here the cheetah started to run," Jon pointed out. "He probably thought he could catch some animal. But if he was raised in captivity, he wouldn't have learned from his mother how to pounce and kill."

Sure enough, after about one hundred meters, we saw where Duma slowed down. A swerving trail of tracks from a Grant's gazelle showed how the antelope had escaped. We stopped to rest. We could barely make out the camp in the distance. "We'd better not get too far," Dave warned.

We could see a billow of dust and heard the growl of a Land Rover. Jon's dad, along with the animal trainer, soon drew up. "Any luck so far?" he asked.

Jon explained about the cheetah's bungled hunting attempt. "Keep following the tracks," his dad said. "I'll stay close by in the Land Rover." Jon and Kamau each took a swig of water from a bottle his dad passed to them. The rest of us jumped in the Land Rover, and we drove slowly along as Jon and Kamau continued to track Duma.

Soon we came to a hardened black lava flow. It looked like pudding that had boiled over the sides of a pot and turned to stone. Jon shook his head. "Duma hopped up onto the rocky flow, but I can't see any more tracks."

"Me neither," agreed Kamau.

We all got out and cast up and down the lava, dark and littered with pockmarked chunks of pumice and occasional seams of shiny black obsidian. We couldn't find any more tracks.

"Duma!" the animal keeper shouted. "Duma! Come back!"

But Duma didn't listen.

We drove back to the movie set with the bad news. "We'll get the Kenya Wildlife Service to come with one of their airplanes," the director said and ordered one of his underlings to get on the radio. "Without the cheetah, we'll have a hard time finishing the movie. We'll do what scenes we can that don't have the cheetah in them, but we really need that animal. Duma's been in training for several years for this movie."

Satisfied that we'd done all we could, we got ready to go. Jill was saying good-bye to Siana when Matt wandered over to them. "I'm sorry about the cheetah running away," he said. "I'm sure the Kenya Wildlife Rangers will find him. Anyway, it was good to meet you. Take care of Ulimi for me." Siana smiled at him, and Matt blushed.

"A new girlfriend, Matt?" Jon whispered at the car.

Matt looked off dreamily. "No, of course not!" he retorted, but his eyes denied his words.

I awoke the next morning to the clanking sound of my alarm clock. I reached over to bang the tab down to silence the noise, avoiding the broken piece of glass that covered part of the clock face. That had happened another time when I'd hammered the clock into silence. Only that time I knocked the clock to the floor. It must have jarred the innards of the clock as well as breaking the glass because, ever since, the alarm made an odd clanking noise instead of ringing.

I sat up, yawned, and looked at the clock. Only the minute hand glowed in the darkness. I had scraped the green stuff off the hour hand after the clock face had broken, wanting to figure out why it glowed. I'd been unsuccessful in my experiment, but I had created a clock that was better at waking me up. I couldn't tell the exact time without turning on the light in my room, and when I turned the light on, it woke me up. I reached over and switched on the light and looked at the clock again. 5 A.M.! Why had I set the alarm so early? Confused images of filming a movie and searching for a cheetah clogged my mind.

Then I remembered. Today we headed for the plains on a hunting trip. Men only on this trip. Matt's dad had gotten permission to hunt on the game ranch on the Ewaso Ngiro River about sixty miles away in Maasai country.

I jumped out of bed and began rushing around to get ready. I pulled on my favorite pair of cut-off shorts, being sure to put my Swiss army knife in my pocket.

I found Dad in the kitchen with a mug of coffee in his hand. He'd already packed several boxes of food. Our tent and two sleeping bags were stacked by the door. I sat down to eat a bowl of cereal.

A sleepy voice complained, "I want to go with you." It was Craig.

Dad picked him up and explained again. "Craig, you're too young for this trip. We took you on a picnic out to Suswa yesterday. In a few years you'll be old enough for a real hunting trip." Craig grumped his way back to bed.

"We decided to take two Land Rovers," Dad said. "That way if one breaks down or gets stuck, we can get help in the other. Besides, it would have been crowded if we'd all squeezed into one."

I nodded. Just then a car's lights shone in our window. I jumped up. "It's Matt and his dad," I announced. We carried our things out and packed them in the Land Rover. We piled in and headed for Dave's house to meet the others.

Matt and I sat on the hard metal benches that lined the rear of the "Landy," as we called it for short. When we hit a speed bump, Matt and I flew off the seats, banged our heads on the ceiling, and bruised our rears on the corner of the benches. Matt moaned in agony about the hard seats.

"Unroll a couple of sleeping bags as padding," his dad said. We were doing that as we pulled into the driveway to Dave's house where his dad's Land Rover stood ready to go.

"There's Kamau," I pointed out. "I'm glad he could come. This will be his first camping trip."

"Dad, can all us Rhinos ride in the back of our Landy?" Matt asked. "We're just getting it padded and comfortable."

"Sounds all right to me," his dad said. "But we'll need to transfer some of this camping gear to the other car."

We jumped out and helped with the packing. Dave and Kamau got in with us, and we drove to pick up Jon and his dad.

The sun was just starting to spread across the valley in front of us as we left Rugendo. The highland morning chill disappeared fast. It would be a hot day. We banged down a narrow red-dirt road that curled along a steep incline for half an hour before reaching the floor of the Great Rift Valley. Here the road had once been paved, but the battered asphalt looked like a bombing target site. We had another thirty miles to drive before reaching the other side. We passed Mount Suswa where we'd watched the filming the day before.

"Keep your eyes open for Duma," Jon said. "He's probably wandering around out here in the valley somewhere." Our vehicles rocked back and forth as they clumped into some potholes and battled bravely to avoid others. Whenever we hit a pothole, the thick gray volcanic dust would seep into the Landy. We coughed.

"I have an idea," Dave said, pulling out a red bandana. He tied it around his face like a masked bandit from one of my cowboy comic books. "Hey, it works great," he said, his voice muffled. None of the rest of us had bandanas. We followed his example by covering our faces with the front of our shirts, and it became bearable.

Matt tried to get us to sing some songs, but we all felt too uncomfortable. Instead, we hunkered down and buried our heads. After what seemed an eternity, Matt's dad said, "There's Narok town up ahead. We'll stop and fill up the gas tank and buy a soda to drink. That dust made me kind of thirsty. How about you guys?"

"All right!" we shouted and jumped out of the Landy as soon as it had stopped by the gas pump. The attendant pumped the gas with the hand-operated lever.

"Doesn't the pump work?" my dad asked.

"Power cut!" the man answered with a smile, cranking back and forth until sweat beaded his forehead. We all walked into Haji Issa's store to buy a soda. It was warm, but at least it was wet.

As we drank, Dad said, "Well, boys, we're only about half an hour away from our campsite. Think you'll survive the rest of the journey?"

We all started talking at once. "I want impala steaks for supper," Matt said.

"No, I want zebra meat," Jon put in.

"Warthog," I said.

"Anything's fine with me," Dave countered.

Kamau said, "I love *nyama choma*, roast meat. My favorite meat is goat!"

"We're not hunting goats. Some Maasai would kill us if we shot one of his goats," Matt said. "Besides, impala roasted over a camp-fire is even better than goat."

"Can anything taste better than goat?" Kamau wondered aloud.

Leaving Narok, we bounced on down the road for another eight miles before coming to a sign that read Ewaso Ngiro Game Ranch. The *askaris,* or guards, at the gate looked at the letter Matt's dad had from Mr. Davies, the owner of the ranch. They knocked on the door of a small office that stood to the left of the gate. A man emerged who introduced himself as the person in charge. He examined the letter, but didn't seem very happy about it.

"Bwana Davies is away for several days," the head *askari* said, scowling. He looked very official in his dark green uniform with gold trim. "But he told me you might come hunting sometime. You really should have told us you were coming so we could have been ready. But since you're here, I'll let you camp down by the river." He gave some vague directions. "You can only shoot warthog, zebra, impala, and Thomson's gazelle," he finished.

My dad passed out some copies of the Christian magazine he edited. The *askaris* immediately started reading and hardly noticed as we drove past the barrier and into the game ranch.

We soon found a dirt track skirting the edge of the river. After driving about five miles, we arrived at a curve in the river with massive yellow fever trees. We pulled in, and Matt's dad got out saying, "This looks like a great campsite."

"Can we go hunting right away?" Matt asked.

Jon got on his knees, looked at all the animal footprints, and told everyone what kind of animals had trekked to the river the night before. "Here's impala and kongoni and even a giraffe."

"First things first," my dad said. "We need to set up camp, and then we'll decide about our first hunting drive." We unloaded the gear.

"One job you boys can do will be to dig a hole for our bathroom," Jon's dad said. He'd brought along a small bathroom tent. It even had a stool, but someone needed to dig a pit. He handed Jon a *jembe*, or African hoe. Pointing out a spot a short distance from the main camp, he sent us to dig.

The nose-blistering sun beat down so viciously we decided to take five-minute turns. Jon dug first. Then Matt. Then it was my turn. But I hadn't hit the hard dirt more than three times when I heard a sharp hissing sound like a bicycle tire that's hit a thorn. With the *jembe* in my hands, my eyes turned toward the noise, and what I saw under the bush made my blood freeze despite the heat.

CHAPTER FIVE

THE PUFF ADDER

No more than six feet away, a snake as thick and as long as a baseball bat moved slowly toward me.

"Snake," I yelled. Or tried to. Fear tightened my throat and the word kind of croaked out. But the other Rhinos understood, and they started to clear out. With my eyes fixed on the slow-moving snake, I tried to step backward so I could turn and run. But I stepped into the hole we'd been digging and fell on my back.

I don't remember praying, but I know in my heart I screamed out for God to save me. I scrambled to my feet still clutching the *jembe*. By now the snake had almost reached me. In desperation I swung the *jembe* down as hard as I could. God must have timed my swing, because I cut the snake clean in two.

I dropped the *jembe* and ran to join the others. By now the shouting had aroused our dads, and they ran to see what was happening. I ran into my dad's arms and began to cry, not out of fear, but from a crazy feeling of relief that I was alive and the snake was dead.

"I killed it," I sobbed. "I killed that snake with the *jembe*."

My dad just held me for a few minutes. We all walked over to inspect the dead snake.

As we neared the spot, Matt jumped back. "It's not dead!" he shouted. "I can see it wiggling around!" His dad reassured him that dead snakes usually writhed around for a while after they died.

"It's just their muscles twitching," he explained.

We all gathered around the snake. Jon's dad took the *jembe* and picked up the snake's head with it. "Puff adder," he said after a closer look. "They're deadly poisonous, so we can thank the Lord it didn't bite any of you boys. And for your bravery, Dean."

I shivered to think of what had happened. "I didn't feel very brave. I just hit out in terror. I think I'll have bad dreams about it. I can still see the snake in my mind. It seemed like it moved in slow motion."

"That may be because puff adders do move in slow motion," my dad said, putting his hand on my shoulder. "God gave puff adders an extra dose of poison to make up for how slowly they move. Usually they wait and ambush small rodents. I thank the Lord it wasn't a black mamba. That's one of the deadliest snakes in the world, as well as the fastest."

"Look how its mottled brown and yellow skin looks so much like the ground," said Jon, pushing on the dead snake's body. The snake gave one last convulsive twitch, and we all jumped away.

"I think we'd better dig our hole somewhere else," Dave's dad said. "Most snakes live in pairs, and this snake's mate may come here. I don't want to have a puff adder catch me with my pants down." We all laughed at his joke, a bit surprised that a missionary dad could talk like that.

They gave me the honor of having the first cut in skinning the snake. I drew my Swiss army knife out of my pocket and made a long cut down the soft yellow underside. Then, with our dads helping, we skinned it. We dropped the carcass and the head into the hole we'd dug and piled dirt on it.

Matt's dad warned us, "Don't hang around this area too much." He went to dig another hole for our bathroom tent on the other side of the camp.

We carried the snakeskin back to camp and poured salt on the inner side to cure it. We stretched it out to dry, pegging it on a fallen tree near camp.

"We can hang it on the wall of our tree fort when we get back to Rugendo," I said. Everyone was excited to have a real snakeskin in our clubhouse.

"You boys hungry?" called Dave's dad.

"We sure are," we all chimed in.

"Then run around and collect some firewood, and we'll cook up some lunch."

We gathered dead branches from a few old acacia trees that had toppled over near the river. We had to be careful to avoid the two-inch thorns on the branches, but soon we'd collected enough for the fire. Dave's dad had gathered together some big stones and placed them in a small circle. We built the fire inside the circle. As the fire burned down to orange coals, Dave's dad set a big smoke-blackened pot on the coals. "How does chili sound?" he said. Our stomachs rumbled as the chili in the pot began bubbling. Dave's dad handed Dave a big wooden spoon with instructions to keep stirring the chili so it wouldn't burn.

He made up some thick biscuit dough. "Cut yourselves a long green stick each and you can have biscuits to go with the chili," he said.

Within minutes we came back with the sticks. Jon had cut an extra stick for Dave, who continued to stir the chili. We put blobs of dough on the ends of the sticks and baked the biscuits by placing them close to the coals.

Kamau smiled, "I've never cooked bread on a stick before. We buy our bread at the *duka*."

Some of the biscuits got burned on the edges and remained doughy in the middle. But they turned out pretty good. By now camp was set up, and we gathered to eat. My dad prayed, and in addition to thanking the Lord for the food, he gave a special prayer of thanks for watching over us when the puff adder had come. I said *amen* to that.

We filled our stomachs with the food, made extra hot with the chilies Dave's mom had bought at the Indian bazaar in Nairobi. After we'd eaten, Matt asked, "When can we go hunting? I want to go right now!"

"Right now most of the animals are hidden away in thickets to avoid the heat," Matt's dad answered. "But later in the afternoon they come out to feed. Let's go out around four o'clock and shoot something for supper."

"Let's shoot a Tommy," Matt pleaded, referring to a Thomson's gazelle.

"No, a warthog," interrupted Jon.

Matt's dad scratched his head. "Well, we've got permission to shoot either one. Both have really nice, tender meat. So let's toss a coin for it." He pulled out a silver one-shilling piece and flipped it.

Jon called tails and won. I should have told Matt that Kenya shillings come up tails more often than heads. The engraved head of the president is so large that it makes the head side much heavier, so a coin toss usually comes up tails.

"A warthog it is," Matt's dad said, picking his shilling up from the ground and blowing the dust off.

It would be another couple hours until we left. Our dads pulled some camp chairs under the shade of the tree and set up a game of Rook. We Rhinos explored the banks of the river.

Matt led the way. After all, he was our club captain. The river snaked along, cutting its way through the soil and leaving eight-foot banks in places so we had to peer over to see the water, which was as brown as chocolate milk.

"Let's see if we can cross the river," Matt announced after we'd hiked for a while.

"I'm not sure," I warned. "The river's not that far across, but it seems to be pretty deep. And who knows what lives under that water? Maybe hippos, crocodiles, even snakes!"

"Don't be so wimpy, Dean," Jon retorted. "Let's wade across."

"Actually," Dave said, "there's a place back around the bend where we could cross without going into the water."

"What do you mean?" Matt asked.

"I saw a natural bridge made by two trees that had fallen across the river. It won't be easy, but I think we can cross on those trees."

"Well, let's get going," Matt commanded. "You lead the way, Dave."

Dave had a big smile on his face as he led us tramping back down the riverbank. "Here's the place." He pointed to where two of the many yellow fever trees that lined the riverbank had fallen over. "By my calculations, the trees are strong enough to hold our combined weight. And those big branches that reach down below the surface seem to indicate the trunks will be stable and won't twist or fall in." We always listened to Dave's calculations. He thought things through in a practical way.

"Who wants to go across first?" asked Matt. Jon volunteered right away. He scrambled across the fallen trees as nimbly as one of the vervet monkeys that chittered in the trees around us.

"It's easy," he yelled back to us when he'd reach the other side. "And over here I see some small animal tracks. Looks like they're from a dik-dik. I'm going to follow them."

"Wait for us," said Matt, teetering his way across the trees. That's the way Matt was. Never afraid of anything and always going into any new adventure full speed ahead. Dave followed, taking careful, measured steps as if he'd calculated exactly where to set each foot. Kamau scampered across, sure-footed as a goat on a rocky cliff.

Now it was my turn. How could I tell the other Rhinos I was scared to death? Jon and Matt were already tracking. Dave and Kamau stopped to wait for me. "Come on, Dean," he encouraged. "It's not that hard. Just don't look down."

I wanted to go back to camp, but I couldn't think of any good excuse to leave. So, taking a deep breath, I stepped onto the log. I struggled to keep my balance and did pretty well.

Suddenly Jon's voice ripped through the air. "You guys, come quick! Look what I found."

I looked up, startled, lost my balance, and began to wobble back and forth. Dave said later my eyes grew to double their normal size. I don't know about that. All I remember is desperately trying to keep from falling in the river.

When I knew I couldn't regain my balance, I threw myself forward, grasping onto the tree trunk with my arms. I just held on there, sprawled flat on the log, my chest heaving.

"Dean, Dean, are you OK?" Dave asked. He began crawling out to help me. "Try to crawl across," he said when he got closer.

My arms felt like they were stuck to the log. I didn't want to let go. "Just release one arm first," Dave said, "and crawl across."

Matt's head popped up out of the bushes. "You guys should see what Jon found in . . . What's going on? Are you two all right?"

Dave turned and told him how Jon's yelling had made me lose my concentration, and I'd almost fallen in. As my audience grew, I forced myself to let go of the log and start crawling across. It may have seemed babyish, but I made it.

On the other side, I checked my arms for scratches. "I'll need to put something on these cuts when we get back to camp to keep them from becoming infected," I said.

"Jon's dad can do that," Matt responded. "Boy, I'm glad you're safe. Do you want to see Jon's discovery now?"

I was still shaking but nodded.

"You'll never believe this," Matt said.

CHAPTER SIX

THE ORPHANED DIK-DIK

We followed Matt and soon heard loud buzzing. Bloated metallic blue flies flew around us, thick as volcanic dust. We came from behind a bush to find Jon holding something brown in his arms. The flies swarmed over something squishy on the ground.

Jon said, "Somebody set a wire snare here and caught a mother dik-dik. It's pretty gross. The wire cut through her neck. But look what I found snuggled right next to her. A little baby dik-dik!"

We all looked at the small antelope in Jon's arms. It was barely as large as a rabbit.

"Can I pet him?" Kamau asked, stepping up and stroking the dik-dik's silky brown hair.

"Can you believe it! A real dik-dik!" enthused Matt. "Let's take him back to camp and show our dads. Maybe they'll let us keep him for a pet."

"It's not a baby rhino, but maybe we could have him for our club mascot," I put in.

The other guys liked my idea. We headed back to camp. At the log crossing, Jon went over first with the dik-dik in his arms. I went next, and even though the others laughed, I crawled to be sure I didn't fall in.

Back at camp we called our dads. "Look what we found!" Jon exulted.

My dad was the first to reach us. He took the baby dik-dik from Jon and said, "Well, looks like you boys have found a little skeezix."

"What's a skeeza-whatever-you-said?" asked Dave. "We thought it was a baby dik-dik."

My dad laughed. "It *is* a baby dik-dik. Skeezix was the name of a comic character when I was a kid. The name kind of tickles my tongue, and I call any abandoned baby animal Skeezix until we find a better name."

"Hey, I like Skeezix for a name," Matt said.

I was kind of embarrassed by my dad's story until Matt said he liked the name. So we called our new dik-dik Skeezix.

We spent the next hour fussing over Skeezix, trying to get him to drink some powdered milk we mixed up. He didn't take to it very well, and we didn't have a proper bottle to feed him.

After several attempts to pour the milk down Skeezix's throat, we had more milk on us than in his stomach.

Dave and Kamau rigged up a cardboard box we'd brought food in while the rest of us gathered dry elephant grass to make a little bed. We picked some green grass from the riverbank hoping Skeezix might munch on that. Skeezix curled into a tiny ball and tucked his wet, black nose into his chest.

"Time to go shoot something for supper," Dave's dad called. "Are you boys ready to go?"

"Yes," Matt shouted, answering for all of us. Turning back to the box that held our new mascot, he stroked the little animal.

"Good-bye, boy," he said. "We're going to do a little hunting, but we'll be back."

We all made our farewells, running our hands over Skeezix's silky back. "Look how the hair on Skeezix's head tufts into a point," Matt said, laughing. "It's almost like the cowlick on the back of your head, Dean."

I stuffed my green bush hat onto my head to cover up the cowlick, and we ran to the Land Rover. The day was cooling off, and animals were coming out to feed.

"We need game spotters," Dad said. "Would you Rhinos like to ride on top?" We clambered up the back of the Landy and plopped ourselves onto the black metal roof rack. We bounced up and down on top of the Landy as we drove around looking for an animal for supper. We knew we were after a warthog, but when you're hunting, you sometimes have to shoot what you find. We had to be sure it was something we'd been given permission to kill. So we kept alert, looking for anything we could eat.

We spotted some zebra grazing in a patch of *leleshwa* bushes. Even though we had eaten zebra before, it wasn't our choice of meat for supper. So we kept on looking.

The Land Rover jerked off the dirt path and jolted over the grass-covered plains. "Hold on tight, Kamau," Matt said. "This area is full of small anthills, and that means there will be ant bear, or aardvark, holes."

"Aardvark?" Kamau asked.

"A big brown animal, kind of like a pig. It lives down here on the plains. We don't have them around Rugendo. An aardvark wanders around at night digging out ants with powerful claws," Jon explained. "It leaves behind deep holes hidden in the long grass. We won't be able to see a hole until the Landy hits it. And if it hits one, we're in for one almighty bump! So grab onto something."

Kamau nodded and curled his hand around the roof rack. I tightened my grip on the spare tire that I sat on to cushion the bumps.

"I wonder why our dads came over this way?" asked Dave. "It seems pretty bumpy to me."

"I think I know," said Jon. He knew almost everything a kid could possibly know about animals even though he'd lived in Kenya the shortest time of any of us in our club. It seemed he was born to live in the bush.

"Warthogs like to live in abandoned ant bear holes," he explained. "They back into the holes for protection. I'll bet this plain is full of warthogs."

With this bit of information, we began looking for straight black sticks moving through the yellow elephant grass. The straight black sticks we searched for were actually warthog tails, held erect whenever the animals ran through the grass. In grass this high, it would be the only part of the pig we could see.

Not surprisingly, Jon saw them first. Pointing at two big fever trees with one hand, he slapped sharply on the Land Rover cab's top with the other. We looked where he pointed. Sure enough, we could see three warthog tails moving through the grass. The Land Rover slowed to a stop, and Jon leaned forward and said, "Warthogs off to the right, in line with the two fever trees."

Just then the pigs moved into some shorter grass near the trees and stopped running. Kneeling down, they started digging up some roots with their curved upper tusks. "The warthogs are praying for their food!" Kamau announced. We all laughed at Kamau's description.

Dave's dad, who was driving, headed the Landy on a slow course parallel to the trees. The warthogs stopped eating and looked at us. But Dave's dad kept the car moving in an even rhythm without getting any closer. When we were about even with the pigs, Dr. Freedman quietly dropped out of the car door opposite the animals and slithered behind some tufts of grass. The warthogs kept watching our Land Rover as it slowly moved away. Satisfied we'd left them alone, the pigs went back to feeding.

Looking back from our vantage point on the roof, we could just make out Jon's dad, edging his way closer to get a clear shot. Whispering, we discussed which one he'd try to take out. "Probably the big male," Matt said. "Did you see the size of those tusks? They curved so far they almost made a complete circle!"

"And his mane," I pointed out. "It was so long the hair flopped over from his back and touched his stomach."

Suddenly a terrific crack filled the air. The next few seconds blur together in my mind. The big pig rolled over once in a cloud of dust and then jumped to his feet and sprinted through the grass, his stick-like tail the only part of him we could see. The other two pigs crashed away as well. Dr. Freedman leaped up and shouted, "Let's follow him. I must have only winged him." Dave's dad stepped on the gas and turned back, picked up Dr. Freedman, and then hit the gas, slashing through the grass in pursuit of the wounded warthog.

We could just see the tail now as it zigzagged and slowed. "Your dad got a good piece of him," Dave said to Jon. "I can see a blood trail." But Jon was disgusted that his dad hadn't dropped the pig with one shot. We always bragged about what good hunters our dads were. And for Jon, the best bushman in the club, it was even more embarrassing that his dad had only wounded a big fat pig. He mumbled something about how his dad should have squeezed the trigger instead of jerking it.

The pig's tail disappeared. "The warthog must have gone down," Jon announced. He had a hopeful look on his face. Maybe the pig would die from one bullet after all.

The next thing I remember is the Land Rover slamming to a complete stop. The spare tire I was gripping lifted up with the force of the blow, and I found myself flying in the air over the hood of the Land Rover and landing heavily in the grass.

I vaguely remember my dad kneeling down next to me asking if I was all right. I nodded, but there was a stabbing pain in my side and I couldn't make myself move. Dr. Freedman did a quick examination before allowing my dad to pick me up. All my bones were in one piece, but I winced when he touched my side.

"You may have bruised a kidney," Dr. Freedman said. "We'll have to watch that. But your back and neck are OK, and you have no broken bones."

My dad lifted me gently and said, "We drove smack into an anthill camouflaged by bushes. It stopped us like a cement wall."

The other guys had been holding onto the roof rack, so they didn't fall off. I had been grasping the spare tire, but it was not tied to the roof rack. "I guess it makes a difference what you're holding on to," I said ruefully.

"You're right," my dad said. "You know, that would make a good sermon illustration about how having faith doesn't help if the object of our faith isn't God. You had a firm grip on the tire, but it let you down because it wasn't anchored to the roof." His brow furrowed as he thought about it. "Many people trust in things or money or other gods to save them. They believe and have sincere faith. But their faith is in the wrong thing, just like you holding tightly to your tire."

"Enough, Dad," I interrupted. "It's not time for a sermon."

He smiled. "You're right. I'm sorry."

Once Dr. Freedman said I wasn't badly hurt, the others rushed through the grass to find the warthog. Jon had marked the spot where he'd last seen the tail and found the dead pig. He called everyone over with pride. "Here it is, and my dad hit him with a perfect shot in the heart." I wanted to see, so my dad helped, and I limped to join the others. Sure enough, it was a perfect heart shot.

"How'd he run so far?" Matt asked. The men shrugged.

"Sometimes animals do that," Jon's dad said. "Maybe it's just the nervous system working. Or it takes an animal a few minutes to realize it's dead. But whatever it is, we've got our supper."

I watched as the others began to cut up the warthog into steaks. Jon looked up at his dad, no longer embarrassed. "That was a great shot, Dad! Can I keep the tusks?"

Jon's dad put an arm on his shoulder and squeezed it. "You sure can," he said.

We left the warthog guts in the grass for the hyenas, packed the meat into the back of the Land Rover and headed to camp for warthog steaks roasted over the campfire.

"Something's wrong," Matt said as soon as we drove into camp.

CHAPTER SEVEN

THIEVES IN THE CAMP

We all looked in disbelief. Tent flaps waved in the breeze. The cook tent had collapsed on its poles, and empty cardboard boxes were scattered around. The Land Rover jerked to a stop, and we all jumped out.

"Our food has been ransacked," my dad said. "There are only a few boxes of cereal left, and they've been partially dumped out."

"Our sleeping bags are gone, too," Jon said after inspecting our tent.

We looked around, everyone reporting on our losses. We came back to the Land Rover. Matt's dad looked at all of us seriously. "Looks like we've been cleaned out, boys," he said. "We can thank the Lord our money and licenses and important things like that were in the car with us. Even though we all feel pretty bad about losing our stuff, let's stop and pray and thank God that we're safe, that we have money to get home, and that they didn't damage the second Land Rover we left here."

It sounded pretty strange to me to stop and thank God when something like a robbery had just happened, but our dads started praying. And as we stood there with our eyes closed, listening to the prayers, we began to appreciate how good God was. My dad prayed about creation and all the things that surrounded us to remind us of his greatness. He prayed about how sin in the world caused problems like robberies. When they finished praying, our stuff was still gone, but I felt better.

"We do have our warthog for supper," Dave's dad said. "But we might have to cut our trip short. It's going to be pretty uncomfortable sleeping with no sleeping bags. You boys get some more wood, and we'll have *nyama choma*, roast meat, for supper."

"I can't wait to eat *nyama choma*," Kamau said with a smile. "I hope roast warthog tastes as good as goat." We scattered to get some wood. I couldn't go as fast as the others because my side still ached from falling off the Land Rover, but I picked up small twigs to get the fire started. As I hobbled along, I found one of our cardboard boxes. I kicked it, and some grass flew out of it. Grass! This box had been the one in which we'd left Skeezix.

"Skeezix!" I shouted. "Oh, no! We've lost Skeezix!" The others came running. In our confusion over the robbery, none of us had remembered our new pet dik-dik.

When all four of us were together, Matt kicked the box over again. "We've lost our new club mascot," he said. "We'd better do something to get him back."

At the campfire we cut pieces of meat, put them on green sticks, and held them over the coals. The meat was tender and juicy. Even without salt, which had been stolen along with everything else, we wolfed it down.

"This is good meat," Kamau said. "But goat is still my favorite."

"Maybe tomorrow we'll shoot a goat for you instead of a wild animal," my dad teased.

After supper, we sat around the campfire and discussed what we would do. None of us boys wanted to go home the next day. We decided to see how we slept that night. If we managed OK, we would think about staying the next two days as we'd planned. Our dads would drive to the gate of the Game Ranch in the morning, report the robbery, and see if they could buy some food supplies at one of the *dukas,* or shops, near the gate.

We began to sing songs by the campfire, led by Jon's dad who had a deep bass voice. First we sang some old cowboy songs my dad taught us, like "Tumbling Tumbleweeds" and "Cool Water." Later we drifted into some Christian choruses.

"Lie on your backs for the next song," Jon's dad said. We laid back, and he started out in his rich voice, "In the stars his handiwork I see, On the wind he speaks with majesty. . . ." Shivers ran up my spine singing about God creating the stars while looking up at the thick white blanket that made the Milky Way. The Southern Cross lit up the horizon. The sky was a glut of stars. After that song, our problems seemed pretty small.

We paused and heard a *Whoo-oo-up!* in the distance.

Kamau's head jerked. "What's that?" he asked.

"Hyenas," Jon said. "I wonder if they're eating what's left of our warthog."

"Could be," his dad said.

We felt sleepy, so we began to get ready for bed. Dave's dad went to each of the Land Rovers to get the emergency flashlights out of the glove compartments so we could have a light in each tent. Soon he called out, "Look what I found!" He pulled out a couple of sleeping bags we'd used in the Land Rover that morning to protect our rear ends. "There aren't nearly enough, but we can sleep close and cover up with these unzipped and spread out."

It's a good thing God saved those sleeping bags for us because it can get cold at night on the plains, even in Africa.

The five of us Rhinos lay down in our tent under one sleeping bag. The closeness stopped us from sleeping right away. "Stop wiggling, Dean," Matt said. "You feel like you're made out of elbows, ankles, and knees." After a moment he went on. "I can't sleep. Why don't we decide what to do about our missing dik-dik."

I didn't have any idea what we could do. I'd given Skeezix up as lost or dead. Another whoop from a hyena convinced me that even if the robbers hadn't taken the little guy, he would make a quick snack for one of those steel-jawed hyenas.

But as I thought about our Skeezix being chopped into two pieces in one bite, Dave began talking about looking for footprints the next morning.

Jon latched onto that idea. "Yeah, if there're no dik-dik tracks, we'll know he was carried away. We can search for footprints and find where these robbers took our mascot. And if there are dik-dik prints, we can follow them. Skeezix is too young to have run far. We should have thought of that tonight!"

"It was too late tonight," Matt said. "It was already getting dark when we got home."

I didn't want to be a wet blanket on the next day's expedition, but I felt kind of nervous. "What if the robbers are armed?"

"Oh, we wouldn't attack them," Matt said. "We'd just find them, and then figure a way to sneak in and get Skeezix back. Anyway, like Jon said, we may discover Skeezix just ran away."

"Well, I think we should ask our dads about it," I went on. It wasn't that I felt scared about tracking through the bush alone. It's just that I felt a bit, well, frightened.

"I think Dean is right," Kamau agreed.

"No way," Matt said. "Our dads would veto the idea right off, and we'd never know what happened to Skeezix. I say we let our dads go off and report this robbery and get supplies. Then we start scouting around using Jon's tracking skills to find out what happened. We can leave a note behind explaining where we've gone if that will make you feel better."

It didn't make me feel any better, but I knew there was no use arguing with Matt. I'd tried before and lost. That's why he was club captain, and I was secretary.

Another hyena whooped, very close this time. "That sounded like it was right next to the camp," I said.

"Oh, go to sleep, Dean," Matt said. "You're an old worry wart."

Just then we heard a shout and the crack of a rifle shot.

"What was that?" Matt asked, jerking up and pulling the sleeping bag off all of us. Scrambling to find our flashlight, we unzipped our tent and peered outside.

"What's going on, Dad?" I called. We got no answer. "Dad?" I called again, fearfully. "Dad, are you all right?"

"Where have they gone?" asked Matt, boldly walking toward their tent. The flap was open, and he shone the flashlight inside. "No one here," he said. We bunched close behind him. None of the others would admit fear, but I could tell from the way we huddled close together that I wasn't the only one trembling.

Jon, always the puzzle solver, examined the inside of our dads' tent. "There's no flashlight," he commented, "so they must have taken the time to pick it up before going out. There's no sign of a struggle. I'm sure they must be OK."

His observations helped calm our growing panic, but the question remained. Where had they gone?

We heard a voice. "Did you get him?"

"I think so," another voice answered. "But I can't find him."

"Dad, Dad!" called Matt who had the loudest voice in our group. "Where are you? What's going on? Are you all right?"

"You boys get back in your tent right way," Matt's dad answered. "We're having a snake hunt."

We scampered back into our tent and zipped it shut. "We don't know exactly what's happening," said Matt, "but I think we should pray for our dads right now." He led first in a short prayer for safety.

I reached for my Bible. "A couple weeks ago we read the most amazing verse. Let me show you." I turned to Psalm 91. "This psalm talks about how God is the one we turn to for safety, just like Matt prayed. But listen to verse 13."

I began reading, "'You will tread upon the lion and the cobra; you will trample the great lion and the serpent.' And look what it says in verses 9 and 10. 'If you make the Most High your dwelling—even the Lord, who is my refuge—then no harm will befall you, no disaster will come near your tent.'"

"Wow, does it really say that in the Bible? It could be talking about us right now," Jon said.

Kamau prayed, thanking God for his promise to keep us safe and asking that God would protect our dads as they hunted for a snake. As we finished, we heard footsteps coming toward our tent.

"Come on out, boys. Everything's all right," Matt's dad called.

We unzipped our tent to see our dads standing there. My dad held a headless snake.

"What happened?" I asked, stepping out. "We heard a shot and then couldn't find any of you." I wanted to hug my dad, but the dead snake dangling in his hand kept me away.

"I was going to use the bathroom," Dave's dad began, "when I heard a hissing sound at my feet and then something banged hard against my boot. I jumped back, too startled even to shout."

"Didn't you see the snake with your flashlight?" Dave asked.

"I'd forgotten the flashlight, but the stars gave enough light for me to make out a snake latched on to the side of my boot. I kicked, and he flew off into the bushes. Its bite hadn't penetrated my foot. I breathed a prayer of thanks for that, but I didn't want to leave an angry snake in the bush by our camp. So I went and got the others."

"We went on a snake hunt," said Matt's dad. He held a large sword-like bush knife called a *panga* in his hand. "Two of us took *pangas* and the other two took .22 rifles."

"I thought I saw the snake and shot, but I missed," Jon's dad said.

"It's pretty hard to hit a snake at night with a .22," Jon said, defending his dad.

"Who finally killed the snake?" I asked. "Did you, Dad?"

He smiled. "Yes, Dean. We were making wide circles in the area where the snake had been thrown at first. I carried the flashlight and the beam caught a flicker of motion. I swung the *panga* and separated the snake's head from its body."

Jon stepped closer to examine the snake. "It's another puff adder. Do you think it was looking for its mate we killed earlier today?"

His dad nodded. "It seems likely."

Dave stood next to his dad. "We prayed that God would protect you like Dean read in Psalm 91. You know, where it says you will tread on a snake."

His dad hugged him. "God sure kept his promises from that psalm tonight, didn't he?"

Once again we prayed, thanking God for guarding Dave's dad as he stepped on the puff adder.

"We better skin this snake," said Jon's dad. "It'll be a reminder to us of this trip and God's promises from Psalm 91." He took his knife and skinned that snake in under five minutes, showing off the skills that made him such a good surgeon. We threw the carcass to one side and stretched the skin next to the one we had cured earlier. Just then we heard a snuffling, dragging noise.

CHAPTER EIGHT

THE POACHERS' CAMP

Matt pointed the flashlight beam in the direction of the noise, and we all saw a hyena loping away, carrying the skinless snake in its mouth. That made my heart start thumping like a church drum.

"God's garbage collectors," my dad laughed. I looked at him and wished I wasn't so scared of things like hyenas and snakes. Then the thought struck me.

"Hey dad, we both killed puff adders today," I said.

"You're right, Dean. God sure gave you courage this morning. I tell you, I was scared walking through the bush tonight, expecting the snake to strike at me any second. But I prayed, and God gave me the strength to go on."

I'd never thought of my dad being scared before. Maybe it wasn't so bad to be scared, as long as I didn't let my fear control me.

"Let's get to bed, boys," Matt's dad ordered. "We have lots to do tomorrow." This time when we got under the sleeping bag, we all felt so tired we fell asleep right away.

I woke up the next morning when Matt's knee punched into my thigh. I groaned and pushed his knee away. That woke him up, too.

"Ooooh!" he complained. "I ache all over. Dean, you had your elbow in my stomach half the night."

"You weren't such a good pillow yourself," I countered, rubbing my thigh. "And my side aches where I fell off the Land Rover." After pulling on cold socks and shoes, we stumbled outside into the sunlight. The warmth of the sun began to ease our aches and pains. Jon's dad looked at my side again and said it was definitely bruised and would be sore for a day or two, but it would heal quickly. The best thing I could do was to walk and move normally since this would loosen up the muscles.

We ate our breakfast—dry cereal and roast warthog—and discussed plans for the day. We all agreed that despite some discomfort, we had managed to sleep. We Rhinos wanted to finish our trip as planned. So the four men would drive back to the gate and report the robbery and buy some food to supplement our meat. We boys would stay around camp until they came back. In the afternoon we'd make another hunting trip, this time trying to find several Thomson's gazelles to deliver to the ranch.

I knew we Rhinos planned to track down the robbers and find out what had happened to Skeezix. I desperately wanted to tell my dad, but I didn't dare. He might forbid us to go, and the other Rhinos would blame me. So I bit my tongue and felt miserable and scared. Even worse, I knew I was deceiving my dad. We agreed to guard the camp and waved good-bye as they drove away.

As soon as they'd passed the first bend in the road, Matt said, "Let's get going, guys. Jon, start casting around for tracks. Dean, write a note telling our dads where we've gone. Dave, you and Kamau fill our canteens and roast a few slices of meat so we can carry them with us for lunch."

I wrote a brief note saying we'd gone searching for Skeezix and attached it to the flap of our dads' tent using a long thorn. By the time I was done, Jon called out he'd found tracks. Dave and Kamau stuffed the cooked meat into a plastic bag, and we ran off.

"I had a tough time finding anything," Jon said. "Our dads tromped out any tracks near camp with their snake hunt last night. It looked almost like a herd of buffalo had been trampling through here. But near the river I found distinct footprints of bare feet. No dik-dik tracks anywhere. My guess is they carried Skeezix away."

"What are we waiting for?" Matt demanded. "Let's go."

Following Jon, we began tracing the trail left by the people who had raided our camp the day before. I prayed silently that God would be with us. I even found myself hoping Jon would lose the trail as he'd done when we tracked the cheetah at the movie set near Suswa. My side still hurt, but the walking had loosened up the muscles, and my pain was more a dull ache.

After about an hour and a half of toiling under the hot sun, Jon suddenly motioned for us to stop. He ducked down. We all copied him, and crawled on our bellies until we lay side by side.

"What is it?" whispered Matt.

"There's smoke ahead, near that cliff." Jon pointed. We looked and saw the wisps of white smoke curling up into the cloudless sky.

"Is it a campfire?" I asked quietly.

"I think so," Jon answered. "But I don't know whose it is. It might be the people who robbed our camp. Or it could be some Maasai herdsmen cooking a goat for lunch."

"Maasai?" Kamau asked. "Maybe we should go back." Kamau

was a Kikuyu and his tribe could still remember times when the Maasai would raid their villages for cattle.

"I agree. We should head back to camp and bring our dads here to investigate," I suggested. Fear created a lump of ice in my stomach.

"We have to find out exactly whose camp this is first," said Matt. "Let's edge closer and see who's making that smoke. If it looks like the guys who robbed us, we'll sneak away and come back with our dads. Now come on, there's nothing to worry about."

"I'm with Dean and Kamau," Dave whispered. I turned, surprised. "Not that I'm scared," Dave went on, "though I don't think Dean and Kamau are scared either. I'm just being practical. Even if we get close, how can we tell if they're the ones who robbed us? I think we're taking too much of a risk. We know where this place is. Let's quietly head back to camp and bring our dads out here."

"Nothing doing." Matt was even more pig-headed than normal.

Maybe all that warthog meat is going to his head and not his stomach, I thought.

Matt went on. "We're going to find out who's making that smoke. If it's the guys who messed up our camp, we'll probably see things like our sleeping bags lying around. We can give our dads a solid report, not some story about seeing smoke. I think you three are just scared. Dave, you and Kamau and Dean can stay here. Jon and I will move closer to see what's going on."

Matt's goading got to me. "I'm coming too," I said. Dave and Kamau flanked my sides, nodding grimly. They wouldn't be left behind either.

Hunching forward, using our elbows as our front legs and dragging our legs behind, we crawled on our stomachs toward the source of the smoke. My green military style canteen that hung on my belt kept banging the ground. Jon flashed me an irritated look and put his finger to his lips for quiet. Sweat dripped into my eyes. I pulled my canteen farther back on my belt so it wouldn't clunk around.

Jon pushed his way under a thick bush. We joined him. From there we had a clear view of the campsite. Three men squatted around a fire, roasting meat. In my heart, I hoped they weren't eating Skeezix. We saw a pile of at least twenty stiff zebra skins under a tarp. A heap of gazelle horns filled another area. A rhino horn stuck out of a partly open gunnysack. Guns leaned against a tree with a jumbled stack of wire and rope snares nearby.

"Poachers," I whispered to the others. "Let's go get our dads and report this to the *askaris* at the gate."

At last, Matt agreed. "We can't do anything except get help. Poachers can be dangerous. Even if we can't tell for sure if it's these guys who stole our stuff, this is definitely a big poaching operation. They need to be caught with the evidence." He paused as if thinking. "You know," he went on, "if we all go get help, these poachers may move on. Or their contact man may show up with a truck to carry away all the animal trophies. Even if the *askaris* come, the poachers will get away. Dean, you and Dave and Kamau head back to camp. Jon and I will stay here and keep an eye on them until you get back."

I started to protest, "But Matt . . ." Just then one of the men by the fire stood up and looked in our direction. We froze. The man spoke to his companions and one walked away in the other direction. The two remaining men settled back onto their haunches by the fire.

"You three had better go now," Matt ordered. Kamau, Dave, and I slipped away. When we were a safe distance, we stood up and started to run back to camp.

Suddenly a gunshot ripped through the air, and we heard shouts coming from behind us where we had left Jon and Matt.

Dave, Kamau, and I looked at each other. "Oh no!" Dave breathed.

I whispered a prayer and said, "We'd better run faster!"

We sprinted through the bush heading for camp and help. I wondered if Matt or Jon had been shot. That thought gave me strength to keep running when my body, especially my sore side, shouted at me to stop and rest. Dave and Kamau kept running, too.

After fiteen minutes, Dave and Kamau slowed down and stopped. I pulled up beside them. "What do you think happened?" I asked between pants.

Dave shook his head. "I don't know, I just hope . . ." He couldn't go on. I put an arm on his shoulder. Dave bit down on his lower lip. I didn't have anything to say. Our friends might have been killed. We had to find our dads and get help.

"I need a drink," I said after a minute of silence. I took a long pull on my canteen, wiped the neck, and handed it to Kamau. The water refreshed my dry throat.

"I've been praying the whole way for God to keep Jon and Matt safe," Kamau said.

"Me, too," Dave answered. "My mind keeps going back to Psalm 91. I'm sure if God kept his promises when he protected my dad from a snakebite last night, he will also be with Matt and Jon now."

I nodded in agreement. "I hope you're right."

A noise in the bushes startled us. "They're following us!" Dave blurted, turning to run. Kamau darted ahead of him.

I joined them, smashing blindly into a whistling thorn bush, forcing an abrupt stop to my flight as the thorns pierced my skin. I turned, expecting to see one of the poachers with a gun or a spear.

CHAPTER NINE

LOOKING FOR HELP

Instead I saw a beautiful orange-red impala buck. The sight of me frightened him as much as his noise had frightened us. He turned to flee but stumbled and fell.

"Dave, Kamau, come back," I called. "It's an impala." I gently eased my way out of the thorn bush, finding a few gashes in my arms and legs, but no deep punctures.

Kamau hung back as Dave and I approached the impala that now lay thrashing wildly on the ground. His back legs were hopelessly wrapped up in a mass of rope and wire. From one of the wires hung a wooden stake, wet and dark from the dirt where it had been anchored. Every time the impala struggled, the wire dug deeper into a bleeding wound in his leg.

"He must have been caught in a poacher's trap," Dave said, examining the animal's leg. "Somehow he managed to pull the trap out of the ground, but now he's so tangled he'll be done for if we don't release him." He reached for the impala's back legs to free him, but the impala used his front legs to scramble away. He fell down again, exhausted and frightened.

"You'll have to hold his front end, Dean," Dave said.

I looked at the impala's curved horns with sharp tips. "How can I hold onto him without getting poked?" I asked.

"Just do it, Dean. We can't leave him like this, but we've got to hurry to get help for Matt and Jon," Dave pleaded.

I reached for the impala's head. He lunged out at me, and his forehead and nose hit me in the chest. Instinctively, I grabbed on between the spread of his horns. I closed my eyes and gripped tighter. If I let go, the point of one of his horns could hit me. He pulled right and left, but when I held him firmly, he submitted and lay trembling against my chest.

"Good job, Dean," Dave said quietly. He pulled out his trusty red Swiss army knife and started hacking away at the rope and wire. Within a few minutes, he had freed the impala's legs.

"He's loose," Dave said. "You can let him go now, Dean."

"How?" I asked.

Unexpectedly, Dave started to laugh. Kamau edged closer and laughed as well.

"What's so funny?" I asked, still clinging to the impala's head with my chest between his horns.

"I wish I had a camera," Dave said, still laughing. "I know it seems funny to laugh when Jon and Matt are in danger, but if you could only see what you look like."

By now the impala had realized its back legs were free, and he struggled to his feet. As he did, I let go and leaped backward, landing on my rear in the dirt.

The impala gave us a puzzled look. He started walking, carefully at first, but then with more confidence. I moved toward Dave. As I did, the impala bounded into the air and leaped through the bush.

"Makes you feel good, doesn't it?" I commented to Dave.

He nodded his agreement. "Now, let's get back to camp and get help."

We started running again, though not as fast as at first. We arrived in camp after about half an hour. Our dads were unloading the food they'd bought.

"Dad, Dad, poachers!" I hollered when I saw him. "Matt and Jon may be caught, may be shot." I collapsed in his arms.

"Dean, what are you talking about?" he asked. "Explain what's going on."

My chest heaved with emotion and exertion, but after I refilled my lungs with oxygen, I managed to explain what had happened. I could tell by the concerned look on their faces that Matt and Jon were in serious trouble.

Matt's dad started organizing things right away. He turned to my dad, "Take Dean and Kamau in one Land Rover. Drive to the ranch gate and bring some *askaris.* Dave, you can lead the rest of us on foot to the poachers' camp where we'll try to rescue Matt and Jon, if they're still alive."

"When you find the *askaris,*" Mr. Chadwick went on, "Dean and Kamau can show you the way to the poachers' hideout where we'll join forces."

"Let's pray before we head out," my dad said, and he led us in one of his efficient prayers that he saved for emergency situations.

Taking three of the guns, the others started hiking toward the poachers' camp. We waved as we headed the Land Rover back on the dirt track toward the gate.

After a tooth-rattling ride, we pulled up in a swirl of dust in front of the wooden house by the ranch gate. My father swung out of the door and ran into the small office. Kamau and I followed and listened to him tell what had happened in rapid Swahili. A two-way radio crackled on a table in the office. A yellowing calendar hung on the wall above the radio. It was two years out of date and encouraged people to have smaller families.

After listening to my father, the *askari* in charge shook his head. "Too dangerous," he said. "You say these poachers have guns. If Bwana Davies was here, we could do something. But we have to report this to the police in Narok and to the Kenya Wildlife Service. When they give us official permission, we can go and arrest these poachers."

Because my dad and the *askari* spoke so fast, I missed some of it. I whispered to Kamau, "What are they saying?"

Kamau leaned into my ear and filled me in.

I could tell my dad was frustrated. "How soon will you be able to arrest these poachers?" he asked.

The man shrugged. "Maybe tomorrow," he answered. "First I have to get a ride into Narok. Then I have to persuade them to come. If they decide it's important, they'll come. Maybe tomorrow. Maybe the next day."

"But these poachers have two of our children," Dad pleaded. "Can't you call them on the radio and get them to come right now?"

"The police insist on a written report before they will come," the head *askari* said. "I'm sorry. Now, just go back to your camp and wait. I will contact the police, and we will take care of this small problem." He smiled and guided us toward the door.

Another *askari* who had witnessed the whole thing looked embarrassed. Once outside, the head *askari* said good-bye, entered his office, and shut the door.

Dad started to get into the Land Rover. "Well boys, it looks like we'll have to do it ourselves," he said grimly.

The *askari* who had looked embarrassed strode over, a determined look on his face. "We'll help," he said softly.

Dad looked at him sharply. "What . . ." he started to ask.

"Drive to that *chai* house over there," he pointed with his chin. "The one with the name Ole Dume on it. You like Kenyan tea, don't you? Order some *chai* and wait for me."

With that he disappeared behind the office to a row of wooden buildings where the staff lived.

We stopped at Ole Dume's *chai* house and sat at a wooden table, damp from many wipings, and ordered *chai*. I loved Kenyan tea—warm, milky, and sweet—but I couldn't enjoy this enamel cupful thinking of the danger two of my best friends were in.

"What's going on with the *askaris?*" Kamau asked my dad. "The head guy said they couldn't help, yet this other one told us to come here and wait."

"I'm not sure," my dad answered. "I just know the second *askari* didn't want his boss to know he was meeting us." He looked at his watch. "If he doesn't come soon, we'll have to join the others and try to rescue Matt and Jon ourselves."

Just then the *askari* stepped into the *chai* house with two others, who were carrying guns. He sat at our table. "My name is Menta Ole Dume. My brother owns this *chai* house. We are both Ole Dume, sons of Dume. After reading the magazines you left at the office yesterday, we realized you were Christian missionaries. I, too, am a Christian. I am saved, and Jesus is my Savior. These other two are also Christians," he said, pointing at his companions. "We want to arrest these poachers and get your sons back."

"But the *askari* in charge said you couldn't go without the police," my dad questioned.

"We believe our boss is the poachers' partner," said Menta with a dark frown on his face. "He works for the white game ranch owner where our job is to shoot some animals for meat. This culling keeps the numbers down so they don't overgraze and ruin the land. Our ranch also serves as a buffer between the wheat farming land and the Maasai Mara Game Reserve. Even though we ourselves shoot some animals, our main job is to protect and control animals, especially the endangered ones like rhinos and leopards. Yet we have suspicions that he protects poachers if they will spit in his palm," Menta went on, referring to the common practice of bribery. "We know this is wrong and have tried several times to catch the poachers ourselves. But it's hard to fight against this man because he has many friends in high places. He has deceived the white man who runs the ranch. We have tried to warn him before, but without proof, he hasn't believed us. Now, with your children in the hands of these poachers, we must act. We've told our boss that we're going out to examine an area where buffalo have broken down a barbed wire fence that surrounds one side of the game ranch. He won't miss us."

We went from the dark gloom of the *chai* house into the brilliant sunshine and climbed into the Land Rover. I sat in the front, straddling the gearshift, and Menta sat beside me. He asked me to describe the place where we'd seen the poachers' hideout. I told him, and he nodded.

"I know the place," he said. "We have often seen the remains of poachers' camps there, but we've never been able to catch them. I think my boss warns them when we are coming."

Menta looked at my dad. "I know a shortcut to this place," he said and began giving directions. There was no road, so my dad had to avoid stones, anthills, trees, and ant bear holes. It slowed us down, but he threaded his way through the bush until Menta told him to stop. "No closer, or they'll hear the car," he said.

We had come around the back side of the camp. In the distance we could see a sheer drop. "The poachers' camp will be below that cliff," Menta said.

I realized we were now above the camp, not below it where we Rhinos had first approached. Crouching, Menta and his two partners ran toward the cliff. "Stay back," my dad warned me. "There may be shooting." He didn't have to tell me twice.

Menta threw himself down behind a large boulder. He peered down over the cliff, gun ready. He stood up and waved us to come on. "They have gone," he called. "There is no one here." Just as he finished saying that, a shot rang out. Menta dropped to the ground.

CHAPTER TEN

SETTING THE AMBUSH

"The poachers are up there," a voice shouted. "I think I hit one."

My dad had thrown me to the ground under him at the sound of the shot, but on hearing the voice, he jumped up. "That's Matt's dad," he said. "I recognize his voice." Dad shouted over the cliff, "It's us! We're not poachers. We're here with the *askaris*. Hold your fire!"

He knelt down by Menta. "Are you hurt?" he asked.

Menta smiled. "No, I just jumped to avoid any more bullets. Your friend can't shoot very well, can he?"

"His son is one of the boys the poachers caught. He's very worried," my dad answered. "I'm sorry he shot at you, but I'm thankful you weren't hurt."

We went to the edge of the cliff and saw Dave and the other three men stepping out from behind some flat-topped acacia trees. Dave's dad put his flattened hand against his forehead to screen out the brilliant sun and called, "Is everyone OK up there?"

"No damage done," my dad said, and we clambered down the cliff.

When we were reunited, Matt's dad explained, "We had just

arrived and were trying to sneak up on the camp. It looked empty, but we thought the poachers might have set up an ambush. We saw someone moving on top of the cliff. Well, I fired without thinking." He turned to Menta and apologized. "I'm so sorry."

Menta smiled and said, "If my son was missing, I would have done the same." He surveyed the camp. "It looks like the poachers ran away with your boys. This camp has been abandoned. They must have realized when someone knew the boys were missing that they'd follow them here. Let's see if we can find any clues to where the poachers have gone."

"They didn't leave with a vehicle," Jon's dad said. "We've circled the camp and found no wheel tracks."

"There were only three men when we watched them cooking a meal," I said. "Even if they made Matt and Jon carry stuff, there's still no way they could have cleared out the camp so fast."

"That's right," agreed Dave. "Right here was a pile of zebra skins. We saw a sack with a rhino horn at the top over there. And remember the stack of gazelle horns and the jumble of snares?"

"And they had a tent and guns," Kamau added. We all searched, but could find nothing. Even the campfire was only a heap of luke-warm ashes.

"It's almost as if you dreamed the whole thing," Menta commented.

"But they were really here," I protested.

"I know," Menta said, soothing me. "I believe you. But these poachers are really clever. Tell me, did you notice whether they had a radio?"

"I didn't see one," Dave answered.

"But we couldn't see inside their tent. They could have had a radio in there," I pointed out.

"Well, we won't learn much more from this camp," Menta said. "And the poachers are such clever bushmen, they will have covered all signs of their leaving so we can't track them from here. We'll have to decide what to do next."

The men gathered together and started discussing their next move.

"I'm hot," I told Dave. "I'm going to sit under that tree growing out of the cliff."

Dave and Kamau followed me. I sat down next to the tree and leaned against a rock. As I did, the rock slid away, and I tumbled backward into a hole.

I landed heavily on my back in thick dust. Dave's voice seemed to come from a distance. "Dean, are you all right?"

I groaned and sat up. "I think I've bruised my side again, but otherwise I'm fine." I looked around. "This is a cave of some kind." As my eyes adjusted to the gloom, I could see what surrounded me.

"Dave, Kamau!" I hollered. "Get our dads. You'll never believe what I've found!"

Moments later, Dave scrambled in next to me, and my dad's head appeared at the entrance to the shaft. "What's down there?" he asked.

"All the poachers' stuff," I answered.

"Yeah," Dave chimed in, "here's that stack of zebra hides and the gunny sack with the rhino horn at the top. Everything. I even see our boxes of food and our sleeping bags."

"Everything except their guns," Kamau added.

One of the game *askaris* climbed down with us and began hauling out the animal trophies. Dave and Kamau and I helped until we had cleaned out everything, except a tangle of wires used by the poachers for making snares. I took one last look around the cave and saw what looked like a small skin in the corner. I walked over to pick it up. I couldn't believe my eyes.

"Look who I've found!" I called. "It's Skeezix!" The baby dik-dik lay shivering, eyes wet, soft and brown. I cuddled him and carried him out of the cave. We covered up the entrance to the hole so it looked like nothing had changed. We all climbed the cliff, carrying the poachers' loot to the Land Rover.

At the car, our dads had a council of war with the *askaris*. Matt's dad wanted to start tracking down the poachers so they could rescue Matt and Jon right away. Jon's dad supported him.

But Menta had another idea. "We can track them," he said. "But they have their guns and your sons. It would almost certainly end in a gunfight, and someone could get hurt. Or they might use your boys as hostages. I think it would be best to set up a guard around this camp. They will return. They left their food here and all their animal trophies. I think they'll return soon. I've never seen such a pile of animal hides and horns. To me, that means they are just about ready to take everything away and smuggle it out of the country."

He stopped speaking, a look of deep sadness on his face. He continued, "To shoot an animal to eat is one thing. To slaughter hundreds so some person overseas can have an animal trophy makes me sick. These poachers would be forced to stop if no one bought their trophies. It's true the poachers do the killing. But it's the middlemen and the overseas buyers who are the real murderers."

Dave's dad responded, "If we wait here until they return, we may be able to catch not only the poachers, but also the merchants who smuggle the goods out—the animal death merchants."

"But Matt and Jon . . ." began Matt's dad.

Menta said, "I know you're worried about your children. I am a Christian just as you are. Believe me, the best we can do for now is to pray for their safety. I am certain these poachers have a time set up to meet the buyers. Do you remember that I told you my boss at the gate wasn't willing to help you because I believe he's involved somehow with selling these animal trophies? I overheard him on the radio last night, and he said, 'One more day and we'll have to pick everything up. Is the money ready?' I suggest we all get in the Land Rover and drive away. We'll come back on foot and set up a guard ready to ambush the poachers when they return. And with the Lord's help, we'll be able to rescue your sons as well."

Everyone agreed it was the best we could do for now. Before we climbed into the Land Rover, we prayed earnestly for Matt and Jon. We drove away, kicking up a swirling dust storm behind the four-wheel drive vehicle.

We hid the car about a mile away and had lunch and drank tons of water. I wasn't that hungry, but the withering heat had given me a fierce thirst. After lunch, Menta divided us into groups, and we followed different paths back to the poachers' hideout.

Dave, Kamau, and I were in one group with all our dads. Menta had chosen our group for what he thought would be the least hazardous duty. We were instructed to sneak up to about a hundred yards of the poachers' camp and hide underneath some yellow fever trees near the river. Menta didn't think the poachers could possibly return from that direction. Yet it gave us a good view of the camp, and we could signal the others if we did see something. The *askaris* covered the other approaches to the camp, with two of them behind the rocks on top of the cliff above the cave.

We separated and made our way to our appointed places. Finding the trees Menta had spoken of, we cleared out some of the bush and hunkered down to watch.

The afternoon sun was hot, and sweat soon dripped down my forehead. A fly buzzed around my head before attempting to land on my nose. I smashed at it, hurting my nose instead. The fly droned off, unsmashed, but wary. Soon his brothers and cousins swarmed all around, making us miserable.

"Does anyone have bug spray?" I asked. No one did, so we endured the flies. As it grew later, the flies got tired of us and left. Nothing had happened. We could not see any of the other groups. We did our best to sit quietly and wait.

I looked up in the sky and saw a sign that is as well known in Africa as the golden arches are in the U.S. "Look at the vultures," I whispered, pointing at the black shapes circling an area a few miles off from where we were hidden. "Something's dead."

Of course, it could be anything from a lion's kill to an animal that died of old age. But in my mind, I saw the poachers. Maybe they'd shot something for lunch. Or maybe… I didn't want to think about it, but maybe… I had a picture in my mind of Jon or Matt's body being picked at by squabbling vultures.

A verse I'd memorized for Sunday school came into my mind. "Cast all your cares on him for he cares for you." I began praying for Matt and Jon. *Dear God, don't let them die. Please God,* I pleaded.

The sun began to go down. My dad passed around some meat he'd carried along, and we chewed on it for a while. We passed a canteen. The sky turned orange as the setting sun shot its dying rays through the dusty horizon. Suddenly it was dark. That's how night comes in Africa—fast. In the distance a hyena whooped.

Still we waited. My dad took out the flashlight so he'd be ready to signal the others if we saw anything. But nothing happened.

My clothes, damp from my earlier sweating, clung clammily to my body as the cold African night crept around us. I shivered. My dad put his arm around me and held me close. I began to feel warmer. What had started out as such a great hunting trip was ending in disaster. I couldn't understand why God let things like this happen. I looked up at the stars starting to light up the sky. I remembered the song we'd sung the night before about God's greatness seen in the stars. *But where is he now?* I shook my head.

Just then the bushes behind us rustled and a branch snapped.

CHAPTER ELEVEN

THE CLOTHESLINE TRAP

I had a hard time swallowing because my heart seemed to have crawled into my mouth for safety. Dave's dad turned quickly and pointed his gun at the area where we'd heard the noise. My dad aimed the flashlight but didn't turn it on. He told me later he hadn't wanted to give away our position in case it was only some animal.

We kept still and listened. I heard a soft thumping noise and a muffled snuffling followed by the words, "I've got to make it. I've just got to make it."

I recognized the voice at once. "It's Jon!" I said in a harsh whisper. "Jon, Jon! We're over here."

Jon tumbled into his dad's arms and started to cry softly. "I can't believe I made it."

Jon's dad said in a trembling voice, "Thank God you're safe. I've been praying and praying."

"I've been praying, too, Dad," Jon answered between sobs.

Matt's dad stood beside them. As the crying subsided, he asked the question we all ached to have answered. "Is Matt OK?"

Jon nodded. "He was when I escaped about an hour ago," Jon said. "I hope he's still fine."

"But what about the gunshot we heard this afternoon when Dave and I left to get help?" I interrupted. "We thought the poachers had discovered you and shot at you."

Jon smiled wanly. "Well, neither of us was hurt, but we did get caught. One of the poachers had gone near the bush where we were hiding. We thought they'd seen us. Matt and I tried to blend into the ground, but there wasn't much we could do. When the gun went off, Matt jumped up and shouted, 'They're shooting at us! Run, Jon, run!'

"We both ran straight into a poacher holding a .22 rifle. He was more surprised than we were! He'd gone hunting for guinea fowl in the bush behind us. Can you believe it? He'd been shooting at birds. He didn't even know we were hiding. We should have stayed hidden."

"It's OK." His dad put an arm gently on Jon's shoulder. "What happened next? Did the poachers hurt you?"

Jon continued, "The man dropped his gun and grabbed us, calling for his friends to come help him. They took us back to their camp and tied us up while they discussed what to do. They asked if others were with us. We said no, but they laughed and said they knew children like us would not be out by ourselves. Besides, they said they'd visited our camp the night before and knew there were others. We told them our dads would come soon with *askaris* to arrest them."

"Did they believe you?" Kamau asked.

"No," Jon answered. "They laughed. They said they knew the man in charge of the *askaris,* so they had nothing to worry about, but they did seem a bit concerned. One kept saying he had children of his own and knew our fathers would come looking for us.

So they hid everything in a cave. They herded Matt and me away to another camp hidden in a thicket of euphorbia trees off that way by some big rocks." Jon pointed, but in the darkness, we could see nothing.

"If they had you and Matt tied up, how did you escape?" I asked.

Jon explained proudly, "After we'd been in the forest for a while, they offered us some tea. We told them we needed to have our hands free to drink. They figured small boys couldn't escape, so they released us, and we drank the tea while they watched us closely. But when they tied us up again I tried something I'd seen in a Mickey Mouse comic book. I took a deep breath as they looped the rope around my stomach and then held my hands tightly, like I was praying, when they tied my wrists. But I held the bottom part of my palms firmly apart. When they finished, I released my breath and put my palms together. My trick worked! The ropes were loose!"

"So you ran away," Dave said.

"Not right away," Jon explained. "As it got dark, I kept wiggling my hands until they were free. I was able to slip the rope holding my waist to the tree down my body. And, finally, I reached down and untied my ankles. I had just started helping Matt when one of the poachers left the campfire and walked toward us. Matt hissed at me to go find help, so I ran. The poacher shouted to the others that I had run away. They said not to try to catch me, that the lions and hyenas would find me soon enough." He shivered at the thought. "I'm so glad I found all of you."

He reached around his dad and gave him a super-glue hug. Suddenly he pushed away from his dad. "I almost forgot! I've got news to help us rescue Matt and catch the poachers. I overheard the poachers talking about their plans to move the skins and horns tonight. A truck is coming from the south. It's scheduled to arrive at about 2 A.M. at the cave where they've hidden the skins and other animal trophies."

On hearing this information, Matt's dad went and got Menta, and they started planning. Menta said, "We were right about them coming back to the cave soon to get their things. But knowing where the truck is coming from will help. There's only one road coming in from the south. We can set an ambush for the truck just as it arrives on that track near the cave. Catching the men who do the smuggling will be more important than catching the poachers. If the poachers appear before the truck does, we can surround them in the cave and rescue your son first. If the truck comes first, we'll get the smugglers. In the dark, we can't hope to catch all of them. I'm sure they'll scatter. Our biggest concern will be Matt's safety. Let's just pray they drop him while they scamper for their own lives. Let's pray now, and then we'll hide ourselves again."

"And this time, we take a more active role," said Jon's dad. "We're moving closer to the cave with you and your *askaris.*"

Matt's dad led in prayer, pleading with God to protect Matt. I kept remembering how God had protected us from stepping on snakes. I prayed in my own heart that God would protect all of us from the arrows (or bullets) that might fly by night.

The men went off to set the ambush for the truck. As we four Rhinos sat there alone, Dave handed Skeezix to Jon. "Look who we found in the cave," he said. Jon was delighted, and he held the baby dik-dik and stroked its silky fur. Suddenly the dik-dik reached up and started sucking on Jon's earlobe.

"Poor thing. He's really hungry," Jon said, gently pulling the dik-dik off his ear. We sat silently as we thought of what might happen in the hours ahead.

"I wish there was something we could do," Kamau said.

Dave didn't answer, but I could see him thinking. Suddenly he said, "There is something we can do. Jon, you stay here with Skeezix. Dean and Kamau, come with me. We have to hurry to the poachers' cave and get the wire we left there. We need to set a trap of our own for the poachers when they run, so we can rescue Matt."

I had no idea what Dave was talking about, but I knew if he had a plan for a trap, he would be able to build it. When Dave built something, it worked. We hurried after Dave and stumbled through the darkness toward the cave.

The half moon had just peeped over the horizon and helped us to see the path. We paused when we reached the entrance to the cave. Peering in, I said, "Dave, it's awfully dark in there."

"You're right, Dean," he answered. "That's why I brought this." He drew a small pen light from his pocket. "It was in my backpack that we got back from the poachers when we emptied the cave." The beam barely lit an area one foot in front of us. But we already had an idea of the layout of the cave and where the snare wire had been left.

We found the wire easily enough. As Dave knelt to start untangling it, he began telling us his plan. "Here, Kamau," he said, "hold this end of the wire while I get it loose from this stick. Now, I've been thinking: when our dads and the game rangers ambush the truck, the poachers will probably run for their lives. The punishment for poaching in this country is pretty stiff. Since they'll have Matt with them, I think at least one of them will grab Matt and take him, perhaps as a hostage, to protect himself. So I started to think, where would I run if I were a surprised and frightened poacher?"

"Where *would* you run if you were a poacher?" I asked as I pulled another bit of wire loose. The piece I held had some animal fur stuck to it. I shuddered.

"The forest," Dave answered. "They'd have to run for the forest where we're hiding. It's the only place with enough shadows and cover for them to escape. There aren't many trees in the direction where they took Matt and Jon. With this moon, if they ran any-where but the forest, they'd be as easy to see as a pinching ant on white socks. They'd never make it. These days, the game rangers shoot to kill."

"I hope they won't," I said, "for Matt's sake."

"Well, anyway," Dave went on, "if they run for the forest, I've come up with a way to stop them and save Matt if we're quick." He began braiding two wire pieces at the ends to make a longer piece and told Kamau and me to do the same.

He continued, "I figure if we put this wire at about four-and-a-half to five feet above the ground and string it from tree to tree along the first row of trees in the forest, it should be about chest to neck high for most of the poachers. It will be so dark under the trees, they'll never see the wire. If they're running fast, it will catch them and flip them on their backs."

I interrupted, "Just like the time I hit old Mrs. Cook's clothes-line at a sprint when we were playing capture the flag at night."

Dave chuckled. "Actually, that's where I got the idea."

"Well, I know it can work. I can still feel the choking I got after hitting that wire with my neck. The next thing I remember, I was flat on my back, and you guys were pouring water on me and arguing about who would have to tell my parents I was dead," I said. I stopped. "But what about Matt?" I asked. "We don't want to hurt him."

"That's the beauty of this plan," Dave said. "Matt's short. If he's being dragged along by the poachers or forced to run, he'll go right under the wire. That's when we'll have to be quick and get to him while the poachers are down."

"You've really got this thing figured out, Dave," I said admiringly. "Just like you always do. But don't you think we should get this trap approved by our dads? After all, we got into this mess by searching for the poachers on our own."

Just then we heard a rock being kicked and voices talking in Swahili.

CHAPTER TWELVE

LEOPARD IN THE NIGHT

Dave switched off his penlight, and we backed against the wall of the cave and tried to stop breathing.

"I'm sure I saw a light," one of the voices said. "But it's gone now. We'd better have a look around."

My knees felt like butter in the sun. I slowly melted to the cave floor. The poachers had come earlier than we expected, and Dave, Kamau, and I were trapped.

Dave knelt down beside me and held my hand tightly. Kamau crouched with us, and I could feel him trembling.

One of the men tripped. "It's dark in here," he said. "Let's use the flashlight."

"No," his companion answered. "The light might alert the poachers, and they'll abandon their plans for a pick up tonight."

Why are they worried about the poachers if they are the poachers? I wondered.

The first man said, "But if the light we saw in here was the poachers, they'll already know their cave has been raided, so it won't matter anyway." And with that he switched his flashlight on. As he swung the beam around the cave, it rested on the wall where Dave, Kamau, and I sat huddled in fear.

"It's the boys," the man with the flashlight said, dropping the barrel of his rifle. "What are you three doing in here? Don't you know the poachers will be coming soon? You could have given away our whole trap."

I was so astonished to see two of the *askaris,* I could hardly speak. Dave stammered, "You... you... you see, we... we... we wanted to get some wire."

"You boys could be hurt," the other man said sternly. "The poachers have guns, we have guns, and it's night time. Your fathers told you to stay hidden and away from here. Now please go back. Now! And let's hope our lights have not disrupted our plans for catching the poachers and the men with the truck."

With that they escorted us out of the cave and back to where Jon had stayed with Skeezix.

"Boy, that was scary," I said shakily after the game rangers left. Dave told Jon how the men had seen our light in the cave and had come to investigate, and how scared we had been that they were the poachers.

"Too bad about your plan for a trap, Dave," I said.

"What do you mean?" Dave asked.

"Well, without the wire, how can we set the trap for the poachers who might run for the forest?"

Dave smiled and produced the wire from under his shirt. "I didn't want to try to explain it to them, so I just took what we needed. In the dim light, they never noticed. So now, you three get busy and help me braid this wire together."

We worked hard to get the wire untangled. When we had it

ready, we walked quietly to the edge of the forest and began string-
ing it from tree to tree. Dave tied it to a branch on the first tree.
After that we wound it once around the next tree at the right height
and went on. Soon we had a section almost twenty yards long
wired and ready. We looked to where the cave was. This would be
the quickest path from the cave to the forest.

We went back to our hideout behind a rock and prayed, asking
God to help us rescue Matt. Then we sat back to wait. Kamau kept
thinking he heard the poachers, but Jon would always say, "No,
that's a bush baby." Or, "That's just an owl."

Shortly before 1 A.M. I heard a noise like a saw cutting wood or
a truck with a loose exhaust pipe. "Do you hear that?" I asked
excitedly. "It sounds like the truck is coming earlier than expected."

I looked at Jon and was surprised to see his eyes wide open in
fear. I had never seen Jon afraid before.

"What's wrong?" I asked. "Are you afraid of the poachers and
the men coming in the truck?"

"That's no truck, Dean," Jon said in a hoarse whisper. "That's
the sound a leopard makes when it's prowling. And it's close!"

"What do you mean, a leopard?" I asked, stepping closer to both
Jon and Dave for protection. "Are you serious? It just sounded like
a truck with a loose exhaust pipe."

The noise cut through the night again, the rasp of a hand saw
ripping through a board. This time I heard a soft grunt after each
sound. This was no truck.

Kamau wrapped his arms around me, and we almost jumped
into Dave's lap. The four of us huddled together with our backs to
a tree. "What are we going to do?" I whispered.

Jon cut me off with a severe gesture to be quiet. I began to tremble. I tried to pray and remembered the verse from Psalm 91, which says, "You will tread upon the lion and the cobra." *Well, God helped us with the snake,* I thought. I wondered if he would also protect us from a leopard. My mind filled with thoughts of being mauled and dragged up into a tree to be a leopard sandwich. *The verse talks about a lion,* I thought. *I sure hope a leopard will count. Surely, God, if you can save us from a lion, you can save us from a leopard. Please, God. We don't even want to step on him like it says in the verse. We just want him to leave us alone.*

I found I had squeezed my eyes shut. I opened them slowly and strained to see through the darkness. I looked at Jon and Dave. They sat silently.

We heard the sawing of the leopard again, this time much farther away. Whatever it wanted for supper that night, it wasn't four Rhinos or our baby dik-dik.

"I think it's OK to talk again," Jon said quietly.

"Thank you, Lord," Kamau prayed. "You know, I prayed for God to save us from the leopard just like he promised in Psalm 91. I just changed the part about the lion to a leopard."

"I prayed the same thing," I said.

"Me, too," said Jon. "And God really answered. Leopards rarely attack people, but when you're alone in the night and it's dark, well, a leopard coughing right next to you makes you a bit, well, nervous."

"I wasn't nervous," Dave said. "I was plain scared!"

We all laughed—a jittery kind of laughter like right after you've survived a twenty-foot slide into a muddy ravine on a hike. We thanked God together and prayed again for Matt's safety.

We sat alert in the dark, waiting, but after about an hour we began to get sleepy. The next thing I remembered was being pushed away by Dave's sleepy voice. "Come on, Dean. Stop lying all over me."

I tried to sit up straight, but after a few minutes I nodded off again, this time on Jon's shoulder. He elbowed me off. "Dean, this isn't the time to snore in your sleep."

"But I never snore," I retorted. "If you want to hear someone snore, you should sleep with my little brother, Craig. Mom says he needs to have his adenoids cut out."

"Well, you sure snored just then," answered Jon. "And now you're doing it again."

"But I'm awake," I protested. "How could I be snoring?" Then I heard it too. "It sure sounds like someone's snoring," I agreed. "But it's not me. I'm talking!"

Jon listened carefully. "It must be the truck," he whispered. We all stood up, fully awake. We pushed our way to the edge of the bushes so we could have a view of the flat area in front of the cave. In the light of the half moon, everything stood out clearly with a pale tinge over the whole scene. I strained to see our dads or the *askaris,* but even knowing where they were hiding, I could see nothing. The trap was well set.

The roar of the truck grew louder, and the harsh glare of headlights danced up and down as it bashed its way up the rutted track.

Suddenly I spotted movement to our right. Four men carrying guns emerged from behind some rocks and strode quickly toward the cave where they'd stashed their skins and trophies. A fifth man led Matt, who stumbled as he tried to keep up. Jon started to lunge forward, but Dave caught him.

"We've got to help Matt," Jon whispered fiercely. "I know what it's like to be tied up and led like a donkey."

But Dave held Jon tightly. "We have to be patient. If we went out now, we'd ruin the ambush and get ourselves caught like Matt. I sure hope the poachers don't go into the cave before the truck comes, or they'll know something's wrong when they see their stuff is missing. It'll get really confusing if our dads and the *askaris* try to catch them just as the truck drives up."

To our relief, the poachers sat down with Matt by the entrance to the cave. One of them lit a cigarette. Its orange tip glowed in the night. A few minutes later the truck stopped and blinked its headlights three times. A flashlight winked back from the cave.

At that moment the *askaris* leaped out of hiding and surrounded the truck.

CHAPTER THIRTEEN

CAPTURING THE POACHERS

Two rangers jerked the door of the truck open. They reached in and yanked out the two men from the front seat. They grabbed them by the backs of their jacket collars and quickly dragged them out of sight behind the truck.

The headlights from the truck continued to glare straight at the entrance to the cave where the poachers sat. From the direction of the lights, I guessed the poachers would have been as blind as an antelope in the road. They must not have seen the men in the truck being surprised and caught. I continued to stare at the cave. A flashlight blinked from the cave. Apparently the poachers were waiting for a further signal from the truck, but the headlights stayed on with a steady beam.

The flashlight blinked again. A poacher stepped forward. He spoke in Swahili to his friends. "They must have forgotten the signal. Or maybe they're drunk again."

He started walking carefully toward the truck. As he reached it, he opened the door and looked in. Turning back to the others, he shouted, "Something's wrong! They're not here!"

The poacher smoking the cigarette stood up. "Look around the back, man. They must be there somewhere. The truck couldn't have driven itself."

As the first man stepped behind the truck, I heard a muffled thump, then a feeble, "Run, man, run."

The second man dropped his cigarette and fired a shot toward the truck. It ricocheted crazily off the metal. He turned and hurtled toward the forest. Within seconds the other three men shot out from under the cliff. One man carried Matt on his back like a pack. A single shot cracked from above the cave, but Matt's dad shouted, "No, don't shoot! They're using Matt as a shield."

The poachers raced toward the forest just as Dave had predicted. We watched, waiting to hear them crash into our wire trap.

As the first poacher approached the line of trees, Dave licked his lips. Suddenly the poacher was into the trees and out of sight. He was quickly followed by the next man.

"Something's wrong!" I blurted out. "The trap didn't work!"

"They're running just to the right of where we strung the wire," Dave said grimly. "I know one way to make the trap work."

And with that Dave ran out of the bushes, shouting wildly and throwing stones. The next poacher shot his gun in Dave's direction, but since he was running, his shot went high. Dave threw himself on the ground. I looked up at the poachers. Sure enough, they had veered to the left. A second later I heard a grunt. The third poacher had hit the wire. He landed flat on his back, and his gun flew into the bushes. The last man, who carried Matt on his back, had no chance to see what had happened. He, too, ran head-long into the wire. It snapped him onto his back, and he fell heavily on top of Matt.

Jon grabbed me and said, "Let's get Matt before the poachers have a chance to recover." As we ran through the bush, Dave and Kamau jumped to their feet and joined us.

"The trap worked, just like I said it would," Dave said excitedly.

We arrived on the scene where both poachers rolled on the ground trying to get air. Matt lay still, moaning. Kamau and I grabbed his legs while Dave and Jon took his shoulders, and we carried him away into the bushes. Jon yelled for our dads and the *askaris* to come since we'd caught two of the poachers.

Flashlights bobbed, and we heard shouts as the *askaris* ran across from near the cave.

"Down by the forest," Jon shouted again.

I looked back. One of the poachers struggled to his feet and started a swaying run into the trees to our right.

"He's getting away," I cried out.

Menta had seen him and sprinted after him.

"Watch out for the wire!" Dave shouted. "Go to the right! The right!"

Menta obeyed instinctively, and with a burst of speed caught up with the poacher and tripped him up with a headlong rugby tackle. The two men sprawled to the ground out of sight in the darkness of the forest floor. Within a few seconds Menta emerged, pushing the poacher in front of him.

The other rangers picked up the second poacher and muscled him toward the truck.

"What happened to these two?" Menta asked as he passed by where we huddled over Matt. "And is your friend OK?"

Matt was still out cold. Dave told Menta about the wire trap, and how the poacher carrying Matt had hit it and had fallen backward on top of Matt.

By now our dads had arrived. Matt's dad bent over and cradled Matt's head in his arms. Jon's dad checked for Matt's pulse, flicked open Matt's eyelid, and shone his flashlight into his eye. At this, Matt groaned again and shuddered.

He sat up suddenly. "Oh man, do I have a headache!" he said. "What happened?" All of us began explaining at once.

"We set a trap to catch the poachers," Dave said.

"Dave threw rocks and yelled, making them run into the wire trap," Kamau added.

"They shot at Dave," put in Jon.

"But the poachers caught the wire under their necks, and it flipped them into the air," I said.

Matt sighed. "I didn't understand a word you all said. It's all jumbled together. But if the Rhinos are here and our dads are here, I guess I'm safe and everything's all right."

We all smiled and nodded. Dr. Freedman said he didn't think Matt had suffered any serious damage from being squished under the poacher, but he'd still watch him for signs of concussion. Matt's dad picked him up, and we started walking toward the truck.

Menta clucked his tongue behind us. "That's quite some trap you boys set up." He plucked the wire as if it were a guitar string. "It's no wonder it stopped those two men. They're lucky they didn't break their necks. How did the other two escape?"

"They ran to the right of the trap," Dave said. "I thought I'd calculated where they'd run, but they surprised me and bolted right past."

Dave's dad put his arm on Dave's shoulder. "You did well, Dave. You stopped two of them, and you rescued Matt."

When we got to the truck, Menta said, "We have the two men from the truck who seem to be the leaders of this poaching ring. We have one poacher who came to the truck to see what was happening. And two more with very sore necks, caught in the boys' trap. I don't think we have much chance of finding the other two tonight, even with the moonlight. Let's tie this group up and put them in the truck. We can pick up your Land Rover on the way back to your camp. I don't trust our commanding officer. We're pretty sure he's the one who gave this group their signals by radio. So we'll take these men to the police in Narok tonight, along with all the evidence that's in your Land Rover."

We all jumped into the truck, and Menta drove slowly back to our camp. On the way they stopped by our Land Rover, and my dad got out and drove it ahead of the truck. At camp we helped the *askaris* pile the skins, horns, and other trophies into the back of the truck. Two of the *askaris,* guns in hand, sat next to the five poachers who were trussed like the impala Dave, Kamau, and I had saved from the snare.

We sorted out our sleeping bags and other gear the poachers had stolen. Menta and his men were ready to leave. "We can't forget to thank God for his protection tonight," Menta said.

Our dads gathered us in a circle, and we each prayed a short prayer of thanks to God. I thanked God for saving us from the arrows and bullets that fly by night. Menta closed with a special praise to God for his power.

The *askaris* drove off in the truck, following another road, which would not go out the main gate of the game ranch. They didn't want to tip off the head *askari.*

We dragged our sleeping bags to our tents. I yawned. "What a day," I said. "I'm tired. But I don't feel like I can sleep. What time is it anyway?"

Dave, who always had on his special digital watch that could tell you what time it is any place in the world, pushed a button, and it glowed an eerie green. "Four A.M.," he said.

"I'm hungry," said Matt. "The poachers didn't feed us very much."

His dad laughed. "You're always hungry, Matt. Hey, we still have warthog meat. Why don't we build up our fire and roast some right now."

My dad said he'd brew up some cocoa to help us fall asleep after we ate, because we were all pretty keyed up.

As we sat around the campfire, Jon's dad began slicing chunks of roast meat. As we munched, I noticed a dappled movement under the acacia trees by the river. "There's something spotted under those trees," I said, grabbing onto my dad's arm. "And we've already heard one leopard tonight."

CHAPTER FOURTEEN

A THREE-LEGGED CHEETAH

"**W**e heard a leopard, too, as we waited at the ambush," my dad said as they quickly herded us into one of our Land Rovers and jumped in after us. Matt's dad turned it on, revved the engine, and flicked on the headlights, hoping to scare the leopard off.

Jon, with his quick eyes, spotted the animal first. He hissed to his dad, "Over there by that tree, Dad. I can see the leopard's eyes glowing green in the light."

We all looked where Jon had pointed. Green eyes glowed in the car's headlights like a horrible version of the Cheshire cat from Alice in Wonderland. The beast stepped out from the shadows.

"That's not a leopard," Jon said. "It's a cheetah. And he's limping badly. Something's wrong with his front right paw."

"He looks small," Dave pointed out. "Maybe he's not full grown."

"Even a juvenile cheetah can be dangerous," Mr. Chadwick said. "Especially if he's hurt in some way."

As the cheetah hobbled closer, we could see that he had no front right paw. There was only a jagged flap of skin where his powerful dog-clawed foot should have been.

Mr. Chadwick tried to scare the cheetah away by honking the

horn, but the animal kept coming—closer and closer. Dave's dad rolled down his window, put his rifle to his shoulder and took aim. The cheetah stopped as if to say, "Go ahead. I've had enough pain. Get it over with."

Slowly, Dave's dad lowered his gun. The cheetah walked right past the Land Rover to the table near the fire where we'd been cutting the warthog. He reached up and tore into the meat we'd left. At last he lay down and started licking the stump of his leg where the paw should have been, before slowly stretching out and going to sleep.

"Well, boys," my dad said, "I think we'll all spend the night in here. I don't want to fight with a three-legged cheetah. Pain makes a big cat grouchy."

"What do you think happened to his paw?" I asked.

Jon answered, "I think he got caught in one of the poacher's snares. The only way he could get free was to gnaw his own foot off."

Dave's dad agreed. "I think you're right, Jon. You can see the ragged skin flap. Poor thing. He'll never survive in the wild. I probably should have shot him, but the look in his eyes was so sad that I couldn't. And now he's sleeping. Well, who could shoot a sleeping cheetah? No, let's just get some sleep here in the Land Rover, and we'll decide what to do in the morning."

"Yeah," my dad replied. "Maybe by then the *askaris* will have returned, and they can help us find a solution. If we leave the cheetah wandering around hurt, he may become a goat killer or even a man-eater."

None of us slept well sitting huddled in the Land Rover. When the sun came up, the cheetah still lay sprawled near our fire.

"I wonder if he's still alive," I said. Matt got the idea of tossing a rock near the cheetah. Quietly he opened the door of the Land Rover and reached down to grasp a grapefruit-sized rock. He threw it and hit the cheetah on the back. The cheetah sat up and looked at us sadly. Matt scrambled back inside the truck and slammed the door as the cheetah came over and sat next to the Land Rover.

"I'm getting hungry," Matt said. "What are we going to do now?"

"I wonder . . ." Dave began. "Do you think this cheetah could be the one that ran away from the movie set?"

Matt's dad scratched his chin. "You never know. It's not all that far from Suswa for a cheetah running in a straight line. And then if it got caught in a trap here, it could have gone looking for some person to help. What was the name of the cheetah at the movie set?"

"Duma," Jon said. "Not too original. It's just the Swahili word for cheetah." As Jon said 'Duma,' the cheetah's ears perked up, and he tried to move closer to the car. But he only had the strength to twitch his tail.

"It's him!" Jon said. "It has to be. Duma was headed in this direction when we lost his trail." He hopped out of the Land Rover and headed for the cheetah.

"Jon, stop!" his dad yelled. "What if it's not Duma?"

But it was too late. Jon had reached out and stroked the cheetah. The animal closed his eyes and began rubbing Jon's leg. "Duma, you poor thing," Jon said. We all piled out to comfort the three-legged cheetah.

Just then the *askaris* drove up in a green four-wheel-drive pickup truck. They started to get out until they saw us surrounding the cheetah. My dad walked over to their pickup and explained the situation to Menta. He nodded. "We have a box trap at our main camp. We can go fetch that. There's a small animal orphanage at Bwana Davies' house where we take care of animals injured in traps. We can get a vet from Narok to come and look at his wounded foot before returning him to the movie people."

"Hey," my dad said, "how'd you get on with the police? Did they arrest the poachers? And does your boss know you're driving his pickup?"

Menta laughed, "I am the boss. At least for now. After we dropped the poachers and the smugglers with the police last night, they told the police my boss was the real leader of their organization. So the police came with us to our camp and arrested him this morning. I radioed Bwana Davies this morning, and he has put me in charge of the Game Ranch until he returns from Nairobi. Now let me go get that trap."

While we waited and sweated in the hot sun, we rubbed Duma's fur. He lay on his side, but kept licking and worrying at his flap of skin. "Poor Duma," Dave said. "I'll bet he never runs away again."

"I'm just amazed we found him way out here. Won't the movie people be surprised!" I said. "But I don't know how they'll finish the movie now that Duma only has three feet." Duma rolled over on his back and looked at us.

When Menta came with the box trap, he and his men jumped out. They put a chunk of raw meat in the trap. Duma smelled it, and within seconds he entered. Menta dropped the door, and his men hoisted the trap into the pickup truck.

"What's to eat, Dad?" Matt said again. It was funny how someone as short as Matt could always be so hungry.

"Are you all hungry?" Menta asked from behind the steering wheel of his truck. We nodded.

"Then get in your Land Rover and follow me," he said.

We piled into our Land Rover to follow in his dust. "Where's he taking us?" Kamau asked.

Our dads just shrugged. Dr. Freedman said, "All I know is that it has something to do with food." After half an hour we pulled up next to a Maasai *boma,* a thorn fence enclosure around a group of round, gray, mud-plastered houses.

"I'm afraid," Kamau whispered to me. "I've never been in a Maasai home before. In the past, the Maasai were enemies of my Kikuyu tribe."

Menta heard Kamau. He smiled as he got out of the truck and said, "Don't be afraid, Kamau. As Christians, we're all one tribe in Christ. Welcome to my *ang*—my home." He called for his wife, who came out the low, open door of the small house in a crouched position before standing up and greeting us. I started to put my hand out and was surprised when she ignored my hand and placed her hand on my head instead.

"That's how adults greet children," Menta said when he saw my confusion. "You're supposed to bend your head forward, and she'll put her hand on your head as a greeting." The other four Rhinos bent their heads to receive the blessing from Menta's wife. A withered old lady came out of the house. She wore black-framed glasses tied together with wire. The lenses looked as thick and as scratched as the bottom of a Coke bottle. Menta introduced her as Kokoo, or grandmother. She hiked her red and white *shuka* over her shoulders, and leaned heavily on a yellowed cane as she shuffled forward to greet us. This time I leaned my head forward, though I wasn't sure she could even tell my head from my hand.

After the greetings, Menta whispered some instructions to his wife, and she rushed off. Kokoo settled herself on a cowhide next to the house and sat contemplating the wonder of having white visitors. She didn't even bother to swish off the flies that landed on her face and glasses.

"I wish I still had Ulimi," Matt joked. "He'd grow big as a dinosaur if he could feast on all the flies around here!"

Menta looked serious. "Flies are a sign of our wealth," he pointed out.

"What do you mean?" Matt asked.

CHAPTER FIFTEEN

DUMA GOES HOME

"**O**ur wealth is our cattle. And where we have lots of cattle, we also have lots of flies. So flies are a sign that we have lots of cattle in our *boma*. Come, it's time to enter my house." Menta ushered us into his home.

We stooped over to enter and found ourselves in a dark, smoky room. Some of us sat on the edge of low cowhide beds, others on short wooden stools. A fire glowed in the center of the room inside three stones. The room had no chimney and only one window about four inches square. Menta's wife soon returned and started boiling some milk for tea. When it was ready, she served it to us in yellow enamel mugs with red roses painted on the sides. Another woman entered with some steaming *ugali,* a thick cornmeal porridge.

"I didn't know Maasai ate *ugali*," Kamau commented. "We always heard Maasai lived on milk and blood."

Menta nodded. "In the past we did mix milk with blood, but times are changing, and we've learned that *ugali* is very tasty."

A third woman came in with a stew made of small chopped pieces of goat meat and potatoes. "My brother slaughtered the goat in your honor," announced Menta.

Kamau's eyes brightened. "Goat! My favorite kind of meat," he said. "But on this trip I've learned that warthog is very sweet as well."

Menta wrinkled his nose. "We Maasai never eat pig meat of any kind," he said.

Tears streamed down our faces from the sharp smoke produced by the *leleshwa* branches in the fire, but the tea was sweet and good. Menta's wife served us large dollops of *ugali* in metal bowls and poured the stew around the edges. We Rhinos were in heaven, wadding pieces of *ugali* into balls and making dip holes with our thumbs before using the *ugali* balls to pick up the rich goat stew.

Ugali is a heavy meal, and soon all of us were full. Menta's brother arrived with four cups of hot liquid. "*Emotori*," he said, offering the mugs only to our dads.

Menta explained, "It's soup made from the goat's stomach. A strong drink, only for men." From the strong smell of the soup, I was glad I wasn't a man.

My dad sipped his, made a slight grimace, commented on how tasty it was, and kept sipping until he'd finished it. Dave's dad and Dr. Freedman battled bravely to finish half a mug each. But Matt's dad couldn't stomach the *emotori*. After a few tries, he asked Menta, "How do I say I'm full in Maasai?"

"*Ataraposhe*," Menta said.

"Well, then, *ataraposhe*," he said, handing the still-full mug to Menta. "And thank you very much."

Menta laughed at him for not being able to drink the soup. "If you want to say thank you in Maasai, you say *ashe oleng*," Menta said.

"*Ashe oleng*," we all said to Menta and his family, and stumbled out into the fresh air.

Menta laughed again. "What's wrong, boys? Too smoky in my house for you?"

"A bit," I answered.

"Come, I want to show you something," Menta said.

We followed him outside of the *boma.* Menta called some of his brothers, and they brought their spears and *orinkas,* wooden clubs with a round knob on the end.

"Let me show you how I used to hunt birds when I was preparing to become a warrior, or *moran,*" Menta said. Pointing at a distant target, he danced forward a few steps and flung his *orinka.* It whistled as it turned end over end, and smashed into the target. He retrieved the club.

"Now you try it," he said. We all tried throwing the club, but only Kamau managed to hit the target. "I practice throwing a club when I watch my family's goats," Kamau explained.

Menta then showed us how to throw a Maasai spear. We tried. Jon did the best, which didn't surprise me. By now our dads had joined us, and they all tried spear throwing and club hurling as well. Finally, it was time to leave.

"I've had a great time," Kamau said to Menta. "At first I was afraid of coming into a Maasai *boma*, but now I know we Christians really are one tribe in Jesus."

Menta smiled and put his hand on Kamau's head. He turned to the rest of us. "Thank you for your part in capturing the poachers. We have one more big job tomorrow. Maybe you can help us."

"What is it?" Matt asked.

"We are going to bring out one of the poachers and have him show us where all their wire snares are hidden. Usually they have lines of them surrounding good water holes. We could find some on our own but not all of them. Anyway, we'll be driving all over the place and uprooting the snares and releasing any animals we find or catching hurt ones to take care of them at our animal orphanage until they recover."

Matt looked at us. "What do you think, Rhinos?" We all nodded vigorously. "Then it's unanimous. We'll help you pull up snares tomorrow."

He stopped and looked at his dad. "Uh, if that's OK with you, Dad. I mean, can we? Please?"

His dad smiled. "Sure. We don't have to be back to Rugendo until the evening. We'd only planned some more hunting, but this project sounds even better. We can all pull up snares in the morning and then deliver Duma to the movie people on our way home."

As we got into the Land Rover, we noticed Skeezix in the corner where we'd shoved him the night before. He looked sick. I picked him up. "Guys," I said, "I think Skeezix is dying."

Menta came up. "Give him to me," he said. "He's hungry. If you try to keep him as a pet, he'll probably die. But I have a mother goat that can nurse him back to health. Then we could keep him in our animal orphanage."

We looked at each other. "Yeah, that would be best," Matt decided for all of us. "Even though we'd like him for a pet, he wouldn't be a very good pet if he was dead. Besides, next time we come out to visit your Ewaso Ngiro Game Ranch we could always visit Skeezix at the orphanage."

Back at camp my dad burped and wrinkled up his nose. "What an awful smelling burp!" he said. "Must have been the *emotori*."

Matt's dad shuddered. "Goat-gut soup. I'm glad I got away without drinking mine. It tasted bad enough the first time. I can't imagine burping it up and tasting it again!"

We all laughed before going into our tents to crash. It had been a very long time since any of us had really slept. "I can't wait until tomorrow," Jon said before falling asleep. "You know, it's even more fun saving animals than it is hunting them."

The next morning we broke camp and joined Menta and his *askaris* for a full morning of pulling up snares. When we had finished piling the tangle of over one hundred wire snares into the Game Ranch's pickup, we stopped by the animal orphanage at the main camp to say good-bye to Skeezix. We found him suckling on Menta's chocolate brown goat. The vet had sewn up the end of Duma's foot, and Duma limped over and began rubbing Dave's leg.

"Since he's tame, you can probably just carry him in the back of your Land Rover," Menta said. We shooed Duma into the Land Rover where we Rhinos had spread sleeping bags on our seats. Duma sat in the middle, and we gave him hugs and pets as the Land Rover pulled out. We waved good-bye to Menta and the others.

As we neared Suswa, we saw clouds of dust. Matt's dad frowned, "Looks like they're taking down their movie set," he said.

My dad pulled out his binoculars. "I think you're right." He smiled. "I wonder how they'll respond when we drive in with their cheetah."

We drove up to the camp, a seething mass of people taking down tents and loading trucks. "Hey, I see Jill and her Cheetahs!" I said. "They must have come down to say good-bye."

"Sounds like you're happy to see her," Matt teased.

"I was just thinking how surprised they'll be to see that we Rhinos have a cheetah. After all, they're the Cheetah club."

Matt's dad swung out of the Land Rover and called the movie director over. Work stopped as the director stalked toward us. "We've decided to call it quits," he said. "Maybe we can work with the footage we have and rewrite the script. The Kenya Wildlife Service rangers have looked everywhere for that cheetah. They even used their airplanes. We've spent a bundle looking, but the cheetah's lost. And without a trained cheetah, we're done."

"Take a look in the back of the Land Rover," Matt's dad said.

The director looked puzzled, but he walked over and stuck his head in the window. "Duma!" he shouted. "You found our cheetah! How?" But without waiting for an answer, he wheeled and ordered, "Stop loading up, everyone. Start setting up camp again. We've got our cheetah back."

Everyone gathered around, including Siana Shane, the actress, and Jill and her Cheetah club. "Can we pet Duma?" Siana asked.

"Before you do that, there's something you need to know about Duma," Matt's dad said.

"What, what? Do you want a reward or something?" the director said, stamping his foot in the dust.

Matt's dad didn't answer that question. "Open the door for Duma, boys," he said. We opened the door. Duma stepped out gingerly and limped on his three good legs toward Siana.

"Duma, what happened?" wailed Siana. Turning to Jill she said, "He's only got three feet!"

"Yes, he got caught in a poacher's snare and chewed his own foot off to escape," Jon explained. "But at least he's alive."

Siana knelt down and hugged Duma. "Yes, at least he's still alive. Poor Duma!"

"I wonder," the director said. "Maybe we can weave this into the script. Duma being caught in a poacher's snare and losing his foot. One of the purposes of the movie is to raise awareness about Africa's endangered wild animals. Yes, I'm sure we can work it into the plot. How can I thank you boys enough?"

Matt answered bluntly, "Maybe you could somehow slip our Rhino club into the story. Have us tracking Duma and rescuing him from the poachers."

"You know," the director said, "that's really a good idea. I've already got some footage of you following Duma's tracks. Yes, I have some ideas of how I could put all five of you into the movie. We'll have to tweak the script. But, yes, it'll be great! Even better than what we had planned in the beginning."

He talked with our dads about the details of when we could come down so they could shoot the film.

As we got ready to leave, Matt leaned his head out the window. "Well, girls, looks like we Rhinos won again," he said.

"What do you mean?" Jill asked.

"Well, I'm glad they chose you to be part of this film, Jill, but you're the only Cheetah in the movie about Duma the cheetah. By my count, there will be five Rhinos in the film, and we'll get to save Duma from the poachers."

Jill's mouth opened as if she would answer. We never heard what she wanted to say because the Land Rover rolled away, sending soft clouds of dust over Jill and her Cheetahs. They didn't seem to mind as they surrounded Duma, rubbing their hands up and down his back.

DON'T MISS THESE RUGENDO RHINO ADVENTURES!

THE POISON ARROW TREE

On a hunt for a genet cat in the Kenyan forest, the Rhinos discover a terrifying mystery—two Kenyan boys lying motionless in the grass, obviously very ill. What happened to the boys? Did someone place a curse on them, as some of the villagers claim? Or is there an even more frightening explanation?

THE CARJACKERS

When vehicles begin disappearing from the village, the Rhinos go on the hunt. Jill and a few girls from school are determined to solve the case before the guys—just to prove they can. It's not long before both groups, the Rhinos and the Cheetahs, find themselves trapped in a life-threatening situation. Will they solve the crimes before things really get dangerous?

THE SECRET OATH

When the Rhinos accidentally stumble across a secret African oathing ceremony, they know they must forget what they've seen . . . or else. But before they know what's happening, Matt is kidnapped right out from under the Rhinos' noses! It's again up to the Rhinos and Cheetahs to discover what happened and rescue their friend.